M.C. Beaton

Agatha Raisin and the

MURDEROUS MARRIAGE

Constable • London

CONSTABLE

First published in the USA in 1996 by St Martin's Press of
175 Fifth Avenue, New York, NY 10010.

This edition published in 2015 by Constable

3 5 7 9 10 8 6 4 2

Copyright © M. C. Beaton, 1996, 2010, 2015

The moral right of the author has been asserted.

A CIP catalogue record for this book
is available from the British Library.

ISBN: 978-1-47212-129-5 (paperback)
ISBN: 978-1-84901-184-6 (ebook)

Typeset in Palatino by Photoprint, Torquay
Printed and bound by CPI Group (UK) Ltd, Croydon, CR0 4YY

Papers used by Constable are from well-managed forests
and other responsible sources

Constable
is an imprint of
Constable & Robinson Ltd
Carmelite House
50 Victoria Embankment
London EC4Y 0DZ

An Hachette UK Company
www.hachette.co.uk

www.littlebrown.co.uk

Chapter One

It was a week before the wedding of Agatha Raisin to James Lacey. The villagers of Carsely in the Cotswolds were disappointed that Agatha was not to be married in the village church but in the registry office in Mircester, and Mrs Bloxby, the vicar's wife, was puzzled and hurt.

Only Agatha knew that she had no proof that her husband was dead. Only Agatha knew that she might be about to commit bigamy. But Agatha was obsessed with her handsome and attractive neighbour, James Lacey, and terrified that if she put off the wedding until she found that proof then she would lose him. She had not seen her drunken husband, Jimmy Raisin, in years. He *must* be dead.

She had chosen the registry office in Mircester because the clerk was old and deaf and totally incurious and she merely had to make statements and fill forms without providing any actual proof, except that of her passport which was still in her maiden name of Agatha Styles. The wedding reception was to be held in the village hall and pretty much everyone in Carsely had been invited.

But unknown to Agatha, forces were already working against her. Her young, erstwhile friend, Roy Silver, in a fit of malicious pique because he felt Agatha had snubbed him over a good public relations opportunity – Roy had once worked for Agatha's public relations firm and had moved to the company which bought Agatha out when she took early retirement – had hired a detective to see if Agatha's husband could be found. Roy was possibly as fond of Agatha as he could be of anyone, but when she had solved her last murder case and he had hoped to gain some personal publicity by being associated with it, Agatha had snubbed him, and as such Roy always felt it necessary to get revenge.

Blissfully unaware of all this, Agatha put her cottage on the market, all ready to move next door into James's cottage after the wedding. From time to time, little stabs of anxiety marred her happiness. Although James made love to her, although they were frequently in each other's company, she felt she did not really know him. He was a retired army colonel, living in the Cotswold village to write military history. There was a privacy and remoteness about him. They talked about murder cases they had solved together, they talked about politics, about people in the village, but never about their feelings for each other, and James was a silent lover.

Agatha was a middle-aged woman, blunt, sometimes coarse, who had risen from poor beginnings to become a wealthy businesswoman. Until she retired to Carsely, she had had no real friends, her work being, she thought

2

at the time, the only friend she needed. So, though possessed of a good deal of common sense and self-honesty, when it came to James she was blind – blinded not only by love but by the fact that, as she had never been able to let anyone get close to her, his singular lack of communication seemed to her possibly normal.

She had picked out a white wool suit to be wed in. With it she would wear a shady hat of straw with a wide brim, a green silk blouse, high-heeled black shoes, and a spray of flowers on her lapel instead of a wedding bouquet. At times, she did wish she were young again so that she could be married in white. She wished she had never married Jimmy Raisin and could be married in church. She tried on the white suit again and then peered closely in the mirror at her face. Her bearlike eyes were too small but could be made to look larger on the great day with a judicious application of mascara and eye-shadow. There were those nasty little wrinkles around her mouth, and to her horror she saw a long hair sprouting from her upper lip and seized the tweezers and wrenched it out. She took off the precious suit, put on a blouse and trousers and then vigorously slapped anti-wrinkle cream all over her face. She had been dieting and that seemed to have taken care of that former double chin. Her brown hair cut in a Dutch bob gleamed with health.

The doorbell rang. She cursed under her breath, wiped off the anti-wrinkle cream and went to answer it. Mrs Bloxby, the vicar's wife, stood on the doorstep.

'Oh, do come in,' said Agatha reluctantly. She was fond of Mrs Bloxby, and yet the very sight of that good woman with her kind eyes and vague face sent a stab of guilt through Agatha. Mrs Bloxby had asked Agatha what had happened to her husband and Agatha had said Jimmy was dead, but every time she saw the vicar's wife Agatha began to have an uneasy feeling that the wretched Jimmy, despite his rampant alcoholism as a young man, might have somehow survived.

Roy Silver faced the detective he had hired. She was a woman of thirty-something called Iris Harris. Ms Harris – not Miss, bite your tongue – was an ardent feminist and Roy had begun to wonder if she was any good at her job or if she specialized in haranguing clients on the rights of women. Therefore he was amazed when she said, 'I've found Jimmy Raisin.'

'Where?'

'Down under the arches at Waterloo.'

'I'd better see him,' said Roy. 'Is he there now?'

'I don't think he ever moves except to buy another bottle of meths.'

'You're sure it's him?'

Iris looked at him with contempt. 'Just because I am a woman you think I cannot do my job. Just because—'

'Spare me!' said Roy. 'I'll see him myself. You've done well. Send me the bill.' And he fled the office before she could lecture him any more.

4

The light was fading from the sky when Roy paid off the taxi at Waterloo station and then walked towards the arches. Then he realized the folly of not taking Iris with him. He should have at least asked for a description. There was a young fellow sitting outside his cardboard box. He appeared sober, although Roy found his tattooed arms and shaven head somewhat scary.

'Do you know a chap called Jimmy Raisin?' ventured Roy, suddenly timid. The light was almost gone and this was a side of London he usually preferred to ignore – the homeless, the drunks, the druggies.

Had the young man denied knowledge, then Roy would have decided to forget the whole thing. He was suddenly ashamed of his low behaviour. But Agatha's stars were definitely in the descendant, so the young man said laconically, 'Over there, guv.'

Roy peered into the darkness.

'Where?'

'Third box on the left.'

Roy walked slowly towards the cardboard indicated. At first he thought it was empty but then, bending down and peering into the gloom, he caught the shine of a pair of eyes.

'Jimmy Raisin?'

'Yes, what? You from the Social?'

'I'm a friend of Agatha – Agatha Raisin.'

There was a long silence and then a wheezy cackle. 'Aggie? Thought she was dead.'

'Well, she isn't. She's being married next Wednesday. She lives in Carsely in the Cotswolds. She thinks *you're* dead.'

There was a scraping and shuffling from inside the huge box and then Jimmy Raisin emerged on his hands and knees and got unsteadily to his feet. Even in the dim light, Roy could see he was wasted with drink. He was filthy and stank abominably. His face was covered in angry pustules and his hair was long and tangled and unkempt.

'Got any money?' he asked.

Roy dug in the inside pocket of his jacket, produced his wallet, fished out a twenty-pound note and handed it over. Now he was really ashamed of himself. Agatha did not deserve this. Nobody did, even a bitch from hell like Agatha.

'Look, forget what I said. It was a joke.' Roy took to his heels and ran.

Agatha awoke the next morning in James's cottage, in James's bed, and stretched and yawned. She turned in bed and, propping herself up on one elbow, surveyed her fiancé. His thick black hair streaked with grey was tousled. His good-looking face was firm and tanned, and once more Agatha felt that pang of unease. Such men as James Lacey were for other women, county women with solid county backgrounds, women in tweeds with dogs who could turn out cakes and jam for church fêtes with one hand tied behind their backs. Such men were not for the Agatha Raisins of this world.

She would have liked to wake him up and make love again. But James never made love in the mornings, not after that first glorious coming together. His life was well ordered and neat – like his emotions, thought Agatha. She went through to the bathroom, washed and dressed and went downstairs and stood irresolute. This is where she would live, among James's library of books, among the old regimental and school photographs, and here, in this clinical kitchen with not a spare crumb to mar its pristine counters, she would cook. Or would she? James had always done all the cooking when they were together. She felt like an interloper.

James's mother and father were dead, but she had met his elegant sister and her tall stockbroker husband. They seemed neither to approve nor to disapprove of Agatha, though Agatha had overheard his sister saying, 'Well, you know, if it's what James wants, it's none of our business. It could have been worse. Some empty-headed bimbo.'

And her husband had said, 'Some empty-headed bimbo would have been more understandable.' Hardly an accolade, thought Agatha.

She decided to go next door to the security of her own home. As she let herself in to a rapturous welcome from her two cats, Hodge and Boswell, she looked about wistfully. She had made arrangements to put all her furniture and bits and pieces in storage, not wanting to clutter up James's neat cottage with them, especially after he had agreed to house her cats. Now she wished she had suggested that they club together to buy a larger house where she could have some of her own things. Living with James would be like being on some sort of perpetual visit.

She fed the cats and opened the back door to let them out into the garden. It was a glorious day, with a large sky stretching across the green Cotswold hills and only the lightest of breezes.

She went back into the kitchen and made herself a cup of coffee, looking affectionately around at all the clutter which James would never allow. The doorbell rang.

Detective Sergeant Bill Wong stood on the step, clutching a large box. 'Got around to getting your wedding present at last,' he said.

'Come in, Bill. I've just made some coffee.'

He followed her through to the kitchen and put the box on the table. 'What is it?' asked Agatha.

Bill smiled, his almond-shaped eyes crinkling up. 'Open it and see.'

Agatha tore open the wrappings. 'Careful,' warned Bill. 'It's fragile.'

The object was very heavy. She lifted it out with a grunt and then tore off the tissue paper which had been taped around it. It was a huge gold-and-green china elephant, noisily garish and with a great hole in its back.

Agatha looked at it in a dazed way. 'What's the hole for?'

'Putting umbrellas in,' said Bill triumphantly.

Agatha's first thought was that James would loathe it.

'Well?' she realized Bill was asking.

Agatha remembered hearing once that Noël Coward had gone to see a quite dreadful play and when asked by the leading actor what he thought of it, had replied, 'Dear boy, I am beyond words.'

'You shouldn't have done it, Bill,' said Agatha with real feeling. 'It looks very expensive.'

'It's an antique,' said Bill proudly. 'Victorian. Only the best for you.'

Agatha's eyes suddenly filled with tears. Bill had been the first friend she had ever had, a friendship formed shortly after she had moved to the country.

'I'll treasure it,' she said firmly. 'But let's put it carefully away because the men will be coming tomorrow to remove all my stuff to storage.'

'But you won't want to pack this,' said Bill. 'Take it to your new home.'

Agatha gave a weak smile. 'How silly of me. I wasn't thinking straight.'

She poured Bill a cup of coffee.

'All set for the big day?' he asked.

'All set.'

His eyes were suddenly shrewd. 'No doubts or fears?'

She shook her head.

'I never asked you – what did that husband of yours die of?'

9

Agatha turned away and straightened a dish-towel. 'Alcohol poisoning.'

'Where is he buried?'

'Bill, I did not have a happy marriage, it was a century ago and I would rather forget about it. Okay?'

'Okay. There's your bell.'

Agatha answered the door to Mrs Bloxby. Bill rose to leave. 'I've got to go, Agatha. I'm supposed to be on duty.'

'Anything interesting?'

'No juicy murders for you, Miss Marple. Nothing but a spate of burglaries. Bye, Mrs Bloxby. You're to be Agatha's bridesmaid?'

'I have that honour,' said Mrs Bloxby.

When Bill had left, Agatha showed the vicar's wife the elephant. 'Oh dear,' said Mrs Bloxby. 'I haven't seen one of those things in years.'

'James is going to hate it,' said Agatha gloomily.

'James will just have to get used to it. Bill is a good friend. If I were you, I would grow some sort of green plant in it, you know, one of the ones with trailing branches and big leaves. It would hide most of it and Bill would be pleased you were putting it to such artistic use.'

'Good idea,' said Agatha, brightening.

'And so you're off to northern Cyprus for your honeymoon. Are you going to stay in a hotel? I remember Alf and I stayed in the Dome in Kyrenia.'

'No, we've taken a villa. James used to be stationed out there and he wrote to his old fixer, a man who used to arrange everything for him, who sent him photographs of a lovely villa just outside Kyrenia and down a bit from the Nicosia road. It should be heaven.'

'I actually came to help you pack,' said the vicar's wife.

'There's no need for that,' said Agatha, 'but thanks all the same. I hired one of those super-duper removal firms. They do everything.'

'Then I won't stay for coffee. I must call on Mrs Boggle. Her arthritis is bad.'

'That old woman is a walking case for euthanasia,' said Agatha waspishly. Mrs Bloxby turned mild eyes on her and Agatha flushed guiltily and said, 'Even you must admit she's a bit of an old pill.'

Mrs Bloxby gave a little sigh. 'Yes, she is a bit of a trial. Agatha, I don't want to press you on the matter, but I am a little taken aback by the fact that you didn't want to be married in our church.'

'It all seemed too much fuss, a church wedding, and I'm not exactly religious, you know that.'

'Oh, well, it would have been nice. Still, everyone is looking forward to the reception. We would all have helped, you know. There was no need for you to go to the expense of hiring a firm of caterers.'

'I just don't want any *fuss*,' said Agatha.

'Never mind, it is your wedding. Did James ever say why he never married before?'

'No, because I didn't ask him.'

'Just wondered. Do you need anything from the shop?'

11

'No, thank you. I think I've got everything.'

When Mrs Bloxby had left, Agatha debated whether to go back next door and prepare breakfast in a wifely way. But James always made breakfast himself. She adored him, she longed to be with him every minute of the day, yet she dreaded doing anything or saying anything that might stop his marrying her.

The fine weather broke the next day and rain dripped from the thatch on the roof of Agatha's cottage. She was busy all day supervising the packing. Then Doris Simpson, her cleaner, called round in the late afternoon to help clear up the mess left behind. Bill's elephant stood behind the kitchen door.

'Now that's what I call handsome,' said Doris, admiring it. 'Who gave you that?'

'Bill Wong.'

'He's got good taste, I'll say that for him. So you're marrying our Mr Lacey at last, and all of us thinking him a confirmed bachelor. But as I said, "What our Agatha wants, our Agatha gets."'

'We're going out for dinner, so I'll leave you to it,' said Agatha, not liking what she felt was the implication that she had bulldozed James into marriage.

Dinner that evening was at a new restaurant in Chipping Campden. It turned out to be one of those restaurants

12

where all energy and effort had gone into the writing of the menu and little into the cooking, for the food was insubstantial and tasteless. Agatha had ordered 'Crispy duck with a brandy-and-orange sauce nestling on a bed of warm rocket salad and garnished with sizzling sauté potatoes, succulent garden peas, and crispy new carrots.'

James had a 'Prime Angus sirloin from cattle grazed on the lush green hillsides of Scotland, served with pommes duchesse, and organic vegetables culled from our own kitchen garden.'

Agatha's duck had a tough skin and very little meat. James's steak was full of gristle and he said sourly that it was amazing that the restaurant's kitchen garden had managed to produce such bright-green frozen peas.

The wine, a Chardonnay, was thin and acid.

'We should stop eating out,' said James gloomily.

'I'll cook us something nice tomorrow,' said Agatha.

'What, another of your microwave meals?'

Agatha glared at her plate. She still fondly imagined that if she microwaved a frozen meal and hid the wrappings, James would think she had cooked it herself.

She suddenly looked across the table at him as he pushed his food moodily about on his plate and said, 'Do you love me, James?'

'I'm marrying you, aren't I?'

'Yes, I know, James, but we never talk about our feelings for each other. I feel we should communicate more.'

'You've been watching Oprah Winfrey again. Thank you for sharing that with me, Agatha. I'm not a

13

talking-about-feelings person, nor do I see the need for it. Now shall I get the bill and we'll go home and have a sandwich?'

Agatha felt so crushed, she didn't even have the heart to complain about the food. He was silent as he drove them home and Agatha felt a lump of ice in her stomach. What if he had gone off her?

But he made love to her that night with his usual silent passion and she felt reassured. You couldn't change people. James was marrying her, and nothing else mattered.

The rain-clouds rolled back on the day of Agatha's wedding. Sunlight sparkled in the puddles. The rain-battered roses in Agatha's garden sent out a heady scent. Doris Simpson was to look after Agatha's cats while she was on her honeymoon. Her cottage stood empty now. Only the elephant and her clothes had been transferred to James's cottage.

Agatha, sitting down to make up her face on the great day, wiped off the liberal application of a brand-new anti-wrinkle cream and then stared at her face in horror. She had come out in a red rash. Her face was fiery. She rushed and bathed it in cold water, but the redness remained.

Mrs Bloxby arrived to find Agatha almost in tears. 'Look at me!' wailed Agatha. 'I tried that new anti-wrinkle cream, Instant Youth, and look what it's done.'

14

'Time's getting on, Agatha,' said Mrs Bloxby anxiously. 'Haven't you any thick make-up you could put on?'

Agatha found an old tube of pancake make-up and put a heavy layer over her face. It left a line where her chin ended and her neck began, so she applied the stuff to her neck as well, and then a layer of powder. Eyeshadow, blusher and mascara followed. Agatha groaned at the resultant mask-like effect. But Mrs Bloxby, looking out of the window, said the limousine to take Agatha to Mircester had arrived.

So much for the most important day of my life, thought Agatha dismally.

The day was fine but with a blustery wind, which snatched Agatha's hat from her head as she was about to get into the limousine and sent it bowling along Lilac Lane, where it settled in a muddy puddle.

'Oh dear,' mourned Mrs Bloxby. 'Do you have another hat?'

'I'll go without one,' said Agatha, fighting back a sudden impulse to cry. She felt that everything was suddenly turning against her. And she dared not cry. For tears would channel runnels through her mask of make-up.

Mrs Bloxby gave up trying to make conversation on the road to Mircester. The bride-to-be was unusually silent.

But Agatha's spirits appeared to lift when the registry office came in sight and James could be seen standing in front of it, talking to his sister and Bill Wong. Roy Silver was also there, feeling virtuous now that he had done nothing to wreck Agatha's marriage, or so he told himself. If Jimmy Raisin wasn't dead, he soon would be. He might have mentioned to Jimmy that Agatha was getting married and lived in Carsely, but Jimmy had been so drunk, so sodden, that Roy was sure the man hadn't really taken in a word he said.

And so they all went into the registry office, James's relatives, and, on Agatha's side, the members of the Carsely Ladies' Society.

Mrs Bloxby took a spray of flowers out of its florist's box and pinned it on the lapel of Agatha's white suit. She noticed that some of Agatha's make-up had stained the white collar of her suit but did not like to say so, thinking that Agatha was already feeling low enough about her appearance.

Fred Griggs, Carsely's village policeman, was unusual in that he liked to walk about the village, instead of patrolling it in the police car. He looked with distaste at the shambling figure of a stranger entering the village by the north road.

'What's your name and what's your business here?' asked Fred.

'Jimmy Raisin,' said the stranger.

Jimmy was sober for the first time in weeks. He had bathed and shaved at a Salvation Army hostel, and then had begged enough money for the bus fare to the

Cotswolds. The Salvation Army had also furnished him with a decent suit and a pair of shoes.

'Relation of Mrs Raisin, are you?' asked Fred, his fat face creasing in a genial smile.

'I'm her husband,' said Jimmy. He stared about him at the quiet village, at the well-kept houses, and gave a little sigh of satisfaction. His sole reason for seeking out his wife was to find himself a comfortable home in which to quietly drink himself to death.

'Can't be,' said Fred, the smile leaving his face. 'Our Mrs Raisin is getting married today.'

Jimmy drew a much-folded and dirty piece of paper from his pocket, his marriage lines, which he had somehow held on to over the years, and silently handed it to the policeman.

Appalled, Fred exclaimed, 'I'd better stop that wedding. Oh, my! Wait right here. I'll get the car.'

The registrar did not get as far as pronouncing James and Agatha man and wife. They heard a commotion from the back of the room and then a voice shouting, 'Stop!'

Agatha turned slowly around. She recognized Fred Griggs, but he was with a man she thought she did not know at all. Even though Jimmy might have been drunk when she left him all those years ago, he had been a handsome fellow with thick curly black hair. The man with Fred had greasy grey hair and a bloated face with

17

a swollen nose and his thin shoulders were stooped. In fact, his figure looked too frail to carry the weight of the large swollen gut which hung over the waistband of his trousers.

Fred went quickly up to her. He had planned to take her aside, to break the news to her tactfully, but Agatha's horrified, mask-like face unnerved him and he blurted out in front of everyone, 'Your husband's here, Agatha. This is Jimmy Raisin.'

Agatha looked about her in a bewildered way. 'He's dead. Jimmy's dead. What's Fred talking about?'

'It's me, Aggie, your husband,' said Jimmy. He waved his marriage lines under her nose.

Agatha was aware of the shocked rigidity of James Lacey beside her.

She looked at Jimmy Raisin again and saw beneath the wastage of the years the faint resemblance to the husband she had once known.

'How did you find me?' she asked faintly.

Jimmy turned around. 'Him,' he said, jerking a thumb in Roy's direction. 'Turned up at my box, he did.'

Roy let out a squawk of fright and took to his heels.

One of James's aunts, a beanpole of a woman with a loud, carrying voice, said clearly, 'Really, James, to have avoided marriage all these years and then to get involved in a mess like this!'

It was then that Agatha snapped. She looked at her husband with pure hate in her bearlike eyes. 'I'll kill you, you bastard,' she howled.

18

She tried to get her hands around his neck, but Bill Wong pulled her away.

James Lacey's voice cut through the shocked exclamations of the guests and relatives. He said to the registrar, who was standing with his mouth hanging open, 'Take us into another room.' He put his hand under Agatha's arm and urged her forward to follow the registrar. Bill Wong brought Jimmy Raisin along after them.

When they were all seated in a dusty ante-room, James said wearily, 'Naturally, the marriage cannot go ahead.'

'Of course not,' agreed Bill. 'Not until Agatha here gets a divorce.'

'Agatha can get a divorce if she likes,' said James savagely. 'But it won't mean marriage to me. You lied to me, Agatha. You disgraced me and I will never forgive you. Never!'

He turned to Bill. 'Try to sort this mess out. I'm off. There's nothing for me here.'

'I was afraid of losing you,' whispered Agatha, but the slamming of the door as James left was the only answer she got.

'Seems like you've still got me,' leered Jimmy.

'You have no claim on her,' said Bill Wong. 'I suggest you get a lawyer and take out an injunction to prevent your husband from approaching you, Agatha.'

'You've done well for yourself, Aggie,' whined Jimmy. 'How's about a bit o' cash to see me on my way?'

Agatha wrenched open the clasps of her Gucci handbag, pulled out her wallet, extracted a handful of

19

notes and thrust them at him. 'Get out of my sight!' she yelled.

Jimmy grinned and shoved the money into a pocket. 'Give us a kiss, then,' he said.

Bill hustled him to the door and pushed him outside and then returned to Agatha.

'Really, officer,' said the registrar, 'I must insist you bring him back as a witness. It appears to me that Mrs Raisin here should be charged with attempting to commit bigamy.'

'The misunderstanding arose like this,' said Bill. 'I was present a year ago when Mrs Raisin received a letter from an old friend in London telling her that Jimmy was dead. Is that not true, Agatha?'

Despite her misery, Agatha was shrewd enough to see the lifeline being thrown to her and nodded dumbly.

'So, as you can see,' said Bill, 'there was no intent to commit bigamy. Mrs Raisin has received a bad shock. I suggest we all go home.'

'Well, since I know you to be a respected officer of the law in Mircester,' said the registrar, 'I will say no more about it.'

Agatha returned to her own home. There was nothing in it but Bill's china elephant and her suitcases of clothes. James had a key to her cottage. He must have carried all her stuff from his cottage and left it. She had asked Mrs Bloxby to tell them at the village hall to have a party instead of a wedding reception. She phoned the removal firm and told them to bring back her furniture and belongings. They said it could not be done that day, but she swore at them so savagely and offered to pay so much that they agreed to be around with the goods as quickly as possible.

Agatha sat on the floor of the empty kitchen and hugged the china elephant and let the tears come at last, carving lines through her make-up. Dimly she was aware that the weather had broken and rain was dripping from the thatch. Her cats sat side by side and looked at her curiously.

The doorbell rang. She did not want to answer it but then heard the vicar's wife calling urgently, 'Are you all right, Agatha? Agatha?'

She took out a handkerchief and scrubbed her face and then went and opened the door.

'Where's James?' asked Agatha.

'He's gone. His car's gone and he left his house keys with Fred Griggs.'

'Gone where?'

'He said something to Fred about going abroad and said he didn't know when he would be back.'

'Oh, God,' said Agatha, her voice breaking on a sob. 'I could kill him.'

'James?'

'No, Jimmy Raisin. Drunken swine. The first good thing I did in my life was to walk out on him.'

'I think if I were you I would feel more like killing Roy Silver,' said Mrs Bloxby ruefully. 'But just think, if it had all come out after you were married, it would have been even more of a disaster.'

'I don't know,' said Agatha wretchedly. 'Perhaps by that time James might have loved me enough to stand by me.'

Mrs Bloxby fell silent. She thought Agatha had behaved badly, and yet sympathized with her motives. And James Lacey *should* have stood by Agatha. Middle-aged bachelors were always difficult creatures. Poor Agatha.

Mrs Bloxby and Agatha sat down on the floor beside the elephant. The doorbell went again.

'Whoever that is, tell them to go away,' said Agatha.

Mrs Bloxby got to her feet. Agatha heard the murmur of voices, then the closing of the front door. Mrs Bloxby returned. 'That was Alf,' she said, meaning her husband, the vicar. 'He wanted to offer you some spiritual comfort, but I told him this was not the moment. What will you do now?'

'I don't know,' said Agatha wearily. 'Take this cottage off the market, rearrange my stuff, go away somewhere until I feel I can face the village again.'

'There is really no need to run away, Agatha. Your friends are all here.'

'You'll start me crying again if you go on like that. I think I'd like to be alone for a bit. Could you tell everyone not to call on me?'

Mrs Bloxby gave her a quick hug and then left. Agatha sat on the floor beside the elephant, staring into space. Three hours later, when the removal firm arrived, she roused herself and let them in. She signed an enormous cheque, tipped the men generously, and then drove to the all-night garage on the Fosse Way outside Moreton-in-Marsh and bought a few groceries.

She wondered whether to call in at Thresher's in Moreton and buy a bottle of something and get drunk, but finding herself suddenly exhausted with misery and emotion, she returned home, bathed and went to bed and plunged into a nightmare-ridden sleep.

She awoke at five in the morning, knowing that sleep would not return and feeling like the character in *Ruddigore* who was glad the awful night was over. She decided to go for a long walk and see if she could tire herself out and so be able to return to bed and sleep some more of the misery away.

Carsely lay silent under the grey light of a watery dawn. The rain had stopped and the air was chilly. The village consisted of one main street with little winding lanes running off it, like Lilac Lane where Agatha lived. With no cars on the roads, the village looked much as it must have done a century ago, with the thatched cottages nestling under the shadow of the square Norman tower of the church. Agatha quickened her step and strode up the hill. She could not think of James Lacey yet or wonder what he was doing. Her mind flinched away from the very thought of him. As she walked on, she

23

began to feel she was walking away from some of her misery and grief.

But it seemed the nightmare was not about to end. For down the road towards her came Jimmy Raisin. He was the worse for drink, swaying and mumbling to himself, an expensive bottle of malt whisky sticking out of his pocket.

Agatha turned on her heel and began to walk down the hill away from him. He came running after her, a shambling, staggering run. 'Come on, Aggie,' he yelled. 'I'm your husband.'

She stopped in her tracks and turned to face him. A red mist seemed to rise before her eyes. She did not even see Harry Symes, one of the farm workers, coming up the hill on his tractor.

When Jimmy reached her, she slapped him hard across the face, so hard that her diamond engagement ring cut his lip, and then, with all her force, she shoved him into the ditch.

She stood over him, her hands on her hips. 'Why don't you *die*!' she panted. And then she ran off down the hill.

One hour later, the police were on her doorstep and she was charged with the murder of Jimmy Raisin.

Chapter Two

They followed Agatha into her living-room: Detective Chief Inspector Wilkes, Detective Sergeant Bill Wong, Detective Constable Maddie Hurd.

Agatha was glad of Bill's presence. Wilkes she already knew, but Maddie Hurd, a rather hard-faced young woman with cold grey eyes, was new to her.

'We must ask you to accompany us to the police station,' said Wilkes after the charge had been read out.

Agatha found her voice. 'Jimmy can't be dead. I belted him one across the face and pushed him into the ditch. Oh, my God, did he hit something and break his neck?'

A flicker of surprise crossed Wilkes's dark eyes, but he said, 'Down to the station and we'll go through it there.'

She suddenly, passionately wanted James Lacey to appear, not because she still loved him, but because he would have taken over with his usual brusque common sense. She had never felt so alone. 'Come along, Agatha,' said Bill.

'I do not think Detective Sergeant Wong should be on this case as he is obviously a friend of the accused,' said Maddie Hurd. Agatha looked at her with hate.

'Later,' snapped Wilkes.

A small group of villagers had gathered outside Agatha's cottage. She wondered bleakly if there could possibly be one more thing she could do which would shame her so utterly in the eyes of the village – first attempted bigamy, now murder.

At police headquarters in Mircester, she was led into an interview room, the tape was switched on, and Wilkes began the questioning, flanked by another detective sergeant, Bill Wong having disappeared.

Gathering all her resources, Agatha said she had gone out walking early because she could not sleep. She had seen Jimmy approaching her. He was drunk. He had run after her. She had lost her temper and slapped him. She had pushed him into the ditch and she had shouted something at him. Yes, she was afraid she had shouted that she hoped he would die. If he had struck his head on something, she was sorry, she had not meant to kill him.

And that seemed straightforward to Agatha, but they took her backwards and forwards through her story, over and over again. Getting some courage back, she demanded a solicitor and then was put in a cell to await his arrival.

The solicitor was an elderly gentleman whom Agatha had picked out a few months before to help her make her will in which she had left everything to James Lacey. He had been avuncular and kind then, the family solicitor from Central Casting with his thick grey hair, gold-rimmed glasses and charcoal-grey suit. Now he looked as if he wished himself anywhere else in the whole wide world but sitting in an interview room with Agatha Raisin.

The questioning began again. 'What more can I tell you?' Agatha suddenly howled in a fury. 'You can't trip me up and get me to say anything else because I am telling you the whole truth and nothing but the truth.'

'Calmly, dear lady,' admonished the solicitor, Mr Times.

'You,' said Agatha, 'have done bugger-all since you got here but look sideways at me as if I am some sort of Lady Macbeth.'

There was a knock at the door. Wilkes snapped, 'Come in.'

Bill Wong put his head around the door. 'A word, sir. Most urgent.'

Wilkes switched off the tape and went outside.

Inside, Agatha's burst of anger had gone, leaving her weak and shaky. Everything was against her. She had attacked Jimmy in front of everyone at the registry office and she had been seen by Harry Symes to attack him that very morning. She was not free to find out who had actually done it should it prove not to have been an accident. Who else could anyone possibly suspect? Who else would want to kill a drunk who normally lived in a packing-case at Waterloo? Only Agatha Raisin.

27

Wilkes came back into the room, his face grim. He sat down again, but did not switch on the tape.

'Where is James Lacey?' he asked.

'I do not know,' said Agatha. 'Why?'

'He did not tell you where he was going?'

'No. Why?'

'I am withdrawing the charge against you, Mrs Raisin, due to insufficient evidence, but must ask you not to leave the country.'

'What's happened?' demanded Agatha, getting to her feet. 'And why do you want James?'

He shuffled the papers in front of him. 'That will be all, Mrs Raisin.'

'Sod the lot of you,' said Agatha, furious again. Her solicitor followed her out.

'Should you need my services again—' began Mr Times.

'Then I'll find myself a decent lawyer,' growled Agatha. She strode out of the police station. They had not even given her a car home. What was she supposed to do? Walk?

'You need a drink,' said a voice in her ear. She turned and saw Bill Wong. 'Come on, Agatha,' he urged. 'I haven't got long.'

They walked across the main square under the shadow of the abbey and into the George. Bill bought a gin and tonic for Agatha and a half-pint of bitter for himself. They sat down at a corner table.

'What has happened is this,' said Bill quickly. 'The preliminary forensic evidence has discovered that Jimmy

28

Raisin was strangled with a man's silk tie. It had been chucked into the field a little down the road. Footprints other than yours were found near the body, the footprints of a man. So the hunt's up for James Lacey.'

'What!' Agatha glared at him. 'They knew all along that Jimmy had been strangled and yet they let me think I might have caused him to strike his head on a rock or something. I've a damn good mind to sue them. And as for James – James murder my husband? *James?* Believe me, the whole experience will have been so vulgar, so distasteful to my ex-lover that all he will want to do is put as many miles between us as possible. So he can't have been hanging around the village to murder Jimmy. That takes rage and passion, and in order to experience that amount of rage and passion, he would need to have been in love with me!'

'Come on, Agatha. The man had a bad shock.'

'If he had loved me, he would have stood by me,' said Agatha. 'And do you know what I feel for him now? Nothing. Sweet eff all.'

'Either you're still in shock or you couldn't have loved him all that much yourself,' said Bill.

'What do you know about it? You're too young.' Bill was in his twenties.

'More than you think,' said Bill ruefully. 'I think I've fallen myself.'

'Go on,' said Agatha, momentarily diverted from her troubles. 'Who?'

'Maddie Hurd.'

'That hatchet-faced creature?'

'Now, you are not to talk about her like that, Agatha. Maddie's bright and clever and ... and ... I think she cares for me.'

'Oh, well, *chacun à son goût*, as we say back at the buildings. Or everyone to their own *bag*. But if they think James did it, they're wasting time. Look, Harry Symes saw me. Didn't he see anyone else on the road?'

Bill shook his head. 'I've got to be getting back. I'll call on you as soon as I hear anything more.'

Agatha thought of asking him for a lift back to Carsely but then decided she had endured enough of the police for one day and went off to get a cab at the rank in the square. Bill went back to police headquarters. Maddie was waiting for him.

'Get anything out of her about Lacey?' asked Maddie eagerly.

Bill told her what Agatha had said, feeling treacherous because Maddie had sent him to find out what he could from Agatha.

'She trusts you,' said Maddie. 'Keep close to her.'

'Are you doing anything tonight?' asked Bill eagerly. 'I thought we could take in a movie.'

'Not tonight, Bill,' said Maddie. 'Too much to do. And don't you want to be around when they pull Lacey in?'

'Of course,' said Bill, banishing romantic pictures of the back row of the cinema and his arm around Maddie's shoulders.

* * *

30

There was only one good thing, thought Agatha wearily as she paid off the taxi outside her cottage – nothing else could possibly happen that day. That was until she turned around and saw a large, tweedy woman standing by the gate.

'Have you forgotten me, Mrs Raisin?' demanded the woman. 'I am Mrs Hardy, to whom you sold this cottage, and I am appalled to see your stuff is still here.'

'I know we signed the papers and everything, but I told the estate agents it was now not for sale,' said Agatha desperately.

'You took my money. This cottage is mine!'

'Mrs Hardy,' pleaded Agatha, 'can we not come to some arrangement? I will buy it back from you and you will make a profit.'

'No, this place suits me. I am moving in tomorrow evening. Get all your stuff out or I will take you to court.'

Agatha pushed past her, put her key in the door, let herself in and went wearily through to the kitchen. How could she, who prided herself on her business sense, have assumed that because she had told the estate agents the house was no longer on the market, all she would have to do was to transfer the money for the sale back to Mrs Hardy?

She glanced at the clock. She phoned the removal company and told them to call the following morning and take her stuff into storage. She then went along to the Red Lion, where she knew they often let out

31

rooms to holidaymakers. But the landlord, John Fletcher, mumbled that he did not have anything to spare and would not meet her eyes. No one else in the pub seemed to want to talk to her.

Agatha abandoned her drink untouched and walked out. There was now nothing left for her in Carsely. The only thing she could do was move back to the anonymity of London with her cats and wait for death. She was comforting her battered soul with equally gloomy thoughts when she turned into Lilac Lane. Her heart began to thud.

James Lacey was getting out of his car outside his cottage. He went round to the boot, unlocked it and took out two large suitcases. Then, as if he were aware of being watched, his shoulders stiffened. He put down the suitcases and turned around.

A weary Agatha came towards him. The rash had gone from her face, leaving it unnaturally white, and there were purple bruises under her eyes.

'Where did they find you?' asked Agatha.

'I hadn't gone far,' he said. 'I stayed the night at the Wold Hotel in Mircester and had nearly reached Oxford when a police car flagged me down. They couldn't hold me. Too many witnesses to the fact that I was far from Carsely at the time of the murder. How's Mrs Bloxby?'

'All right, I suppose.' Agatha looked surprised. 'Why?'

'Well, she found the body.'

'What?'

'They didn't tell you?'

'They didn't tell me a damn thing. They charged me with the murder and then asked me the same questions over and over again, but they didn't tell me how he was killed or who had found him. The bastards let me go on thinking that it was all my fault, that I had pushed him and he had broken his neck or something. Then they said they were dropping the charges because Jimmy had been strangled with a man's silk tie and that there were masculine footprints found near the body.'

There was a silence and then James asked, 'Have the press been bothering you?'

'By some miracle, no.'

'I suppose they'll be all over the village by tomorrow.'

'It won't bother me,' sighed Agatha. 'I've got to leave. I sold my cottage to a Mrs Hardy and, like a fool, I thought I could cancel the sale. But she's moving in tomorrow and I'm out. I went to the Red Lion to see if I could take a room there, but it seems I am still number-one suspect in the village. John Fletcher said he hadn't a room; he wouldn't even look me in the eye, and neither would anyone else.'

'But, Agatha, you told me all about the Hardy woman and that you didn't like her much but she had offered a good price. How on earth could you expect her to change her mind?'

'I don't find myself disgraced in a registry office every day and then accused of murder. I wasn't thinking straight. I just want to get away, from you, from everyone.'

33

He picked up his suitcases and then put them down again. 'I really don't think that's the answer, Agatha.'

'And what is?'

'I assume we both still want to stay here?'

Agatha shook her head.

'You do what you like,' said James, 'but until I find out who killed your husband, despite every proof to the contrary, we are both going to be suspected of his murder.'

'I don't know,' said Agatha wretchedly. 'I've got to get all that stuff of mine moved out and into storage again and then I have to think where I will live.'

'You can move into my spare room if you like.'

'What? I thought you never wanted to see me again.'

'The situation has somewhat changed. I think I will always be too sore at you, Agatha, to ever want to marry you. But the hard fact is that we have worked well together in the past and together we might clear this up.'

Agatha looked at him in wonder. 'I don't think I ever really knew you.' She thought that if he had entertained any feelings for her at all, he would not ask her now to move in on such a businesslike basis. It would have been more human to have been totally spurned and totally rejected.

But she felt she no longer loved him and what he was offering was a very practical solution.

'Okay. Thanks,' she said. 'I think I'll call on Mrs Bloxby. She must be feeling awful.'

'Good idea. Wait a minute while I put these bags inside and I'll come with you.'

When they walked along together in the twilight, Agatha thought that the women's magazines who wrote all that crap about low self-esteem might have something after all. She was walking along beside a man with whom she had shared passion and listening to him complain about the potholes in the road and suggest that they both attend the next parish council meeting to protest about them. Women of low self-esteem, she had read recently, often loved men who were incapable of returning love and affection.

'Do you think I suffer from low self-esteem?' she asked James abruptly, interrupting his discourse on potholes.

'What's that?'

'Feeling lower than whale shit.'

'I think you're miserable because you tried to commit bigamy and got found out and then found yourself accused of your husband's murder. There's too much psychobabble these days. It leads to self-dramatization.'

'Any woman ever struck you, James?'

'Don't even think about it, Agatha.'

Mrs Bloxby blinked at them in surprise when she opened the vicarage door. 'Both of you? That's nice. Come in. What a terrible thing.'

They followed her into the vicarage living-room, which as usual enfolded them in its atmosphere of peace. The vicar, on seeing Agatha, hurriedly put down the newspaper he had been reading, mumbled something about a sermon to write, and fled to his study.

'Sit down,' said Mrs Bloxby. 'I'll get some tea.'

She always looks like a lady, thought Agatha wistfully. Even in that old Liberty dress and with not a scrap of make-up on, she looks like a lady.

James leaned back in a comfortable leather armchair and closed his eyes. Agatha realized as she looked at him that she had not stopped to think for a minute how he had felt over the aborted marriage and the wretched murder. He looked tired and older, the lines running down either side of his mouth more prominent.

Mrs Bloxby came back in carrying the tea-tray. 'I have some excellent fruit cake, a present from the Mircester Ladies' Society. And some ham sandwiches. I suppose neither of you has had much time to eat.'

James opened his eyes and said wearily, 'We have both been suspected of this murder, it's been a long day, and yes, I would love some sandwiches. According to Agatha, we are regarded by the village as murder suspects.'

'Are you sure, Agatha?' asked Mrs Bloxby.

Agatha told her story of trying to find a room at the Red Lion.

'Oh, how sad. We could put you up here. We could . . .'

There was a warning cough from the doorway. The vicar stood there with a distinctly un-Christian light in his eyes.

'That won't be necessary,' said James quickly. 'Agatha's moving in with me.'

'What did you want to say, Alf?' Mrs Bloxby asked her husband.

'Er . . . nothing,' he said and disappeared again.

'You found the body, didn't you?' said James. 'Tell us about it, if it isn't too painful.'

'It was a shock at the time. I did not recognize him,' said Mrs Bloxby, pouring tea into thin china cups. 'Dead people look quite different when the spirit has left. Then he had been strangled, so his face was not pretty. I had gone out for a walk. I was worried about you, Agatha, and I could not sleep.'

Agatha's eyes suddenly filled with weak tears. The idea that anyone could actually lose sleep over her was a novelty.

'At first I thought it was a bundle of old clothes in the ditch, but then, when I took a good look, I saw him. I felt for his pulse and finding none, I ran to the nearest cottage and phoned the police.'

'Was there anyone else about?' asked Agatha.

'No, and it must have happened after you reached home, Agatha, or I would have met you on the road or seen whoever killed him. Of course the murderer could have cut across the fields.'

'We'll just need to find out who did it ourselves,' said Agatha.

'Oh, you've been through so much. Why not leave it to the police?'

'Because we want to know who did it,' said James. 'I've been thinking – what is the etiquette about wedding presents? I suppose we return them.'

'I would just keep them,' said the vicar's wife, 'and

37

then when you do get married, no one needs to bother giving you anything else.'

'We will not be getting married,' said James in a flat voice.

There was a heavy silence. Then Mrs Bloxby said brightly, 'More tea?'

Roy Silver had had a sleepless night. Not usually plagued with an uneasy conscience, he found he was actually suffering. The story of the wedding-that-never-was, spiced up by the murder of Agatha's husband, was all over the newspapers, and some enterprising reporter had found out that he, Roy Silver, had been the one who had alerted Jimmy Raisin to his wife's attempt to marry someone else. The moment he got to his office he phoned Iris Harris, the detective, and asked her to call on him as soon as possible.

He fretted and fidgeted until she arrived. Ms Harris had read the newspapers and listened calmly as Roy said she must find out more about Jimmy Raisin. If Agatha did not kill him, someone did, and that some-one might have some connection with his London background. He could not have spent all those years drinking methylated spirits and stayed alive.

Only when Iris Harris had agreed to work for him again and had left did Roy feel more comfortable with himself.

* * *

Agatha and James stayed indoors most of the following week, only venturing out at night for dinner. The press besieged James's cottage at all hours of the day. It would have been normal, Agatha thought, for them to have discussed their relationship, discussed what had happened, but James talked only about the murder, politics and the weather. He worked away steadily at his military history while Agatha played with her cats in the garden and read books.

At night, she slept in the spare room, strangely undisturbed by any longing for the body asleep along the narrow corridor. The shocks of the wedding and the murder had driven passion from Agatha's mind. She was itching to get started on the murder investigation. Bill Wong had not called and she felt desperate for news. But soon the press would give up and go away to fresh woods and murders new and leave them in peace.

On the morning the doorbell finally stopped ringing and the telephone at last was silent, Agatha decided to go to Mircester to try to see Bill Wong. James said he would stay and work at his writing.

On arriving at police headquarters, Agatha found out it was Bill's day off. She wondered whether to call at his home, but decided against it. He lived with his parents and Agatha found them rather intimidating. So she shopped for a new dress, although she did not need one, and for a new lipstick to add to the twenty or so already cluttering up the shelf in James's bathroom. The lipstick promised to make 'lips full and luscious as never before'.

Agatha, who never believed a word of most advertisements, was a sucker for any cosmetic promotion. Hope sprang eternal and she believed every word until she tried it out. She decided to treat herself to a bar lunch in the George, but she would put on that lipstick first.

She went into the pub toilet, read all the claims of the lipstick as if reading her horoscope, unscrewed it and decided to apply it.

She had it halfway to her mouth when a familiar voice said, 'But Agatha's my friend. It makes it difficult.'

Agatha turned round, startled. Then she remembered the odd acoustics of the George. There was a fanlight window above the door, usually open, as it was that day, so that any diners sitting at a table on the other side of the door almost sounded as if they were in the toilet itself.

That's Bill Wong, thought Agatha with a smile. She tucked the lipstick away in her handbag, unapplied, and made for the door.

Then she heard a female voice saying, 'As far as I am concerned, Bill, Agatha Raisin is still a murder suspect. She could easily have put on a pair of men's shoes to baffle Forensic, and she's strong enough to strangle a man. Beefy sort of woman.'

Agatha stood stock-still, her mouth a little open, her hand stretched out to the handle of the door.

'Look, Maddie' – Bill's voice again – 'I know Agatha, and she would not murder anyone. She's a lady.'

40

'Oh, come on, Bill, the way you go on about the old trout, one would think you were her toy-boy. And ladies don't go around belting chaps over the face.'

'What you are asking me to do is spy on Agatha,' said Bill, 'and I don't like it.'

Maddie Hurd's voice came sharp and clear. 'All I'm asking you to do is police work, Bill. If she didn't do it, and Lacey didn't do it, then the clues as to who did lie in Jimmy Raisin's background. I mean, I'm surprised you haven't called on her before this.'

'I would have done,' said Bill, 'if you hadn't made me feel like a traitor.'

Maddie's voice softened. 'You know I wouldn't ask you to do anything bad, Bill. Did you enjoy last night?'

Bill's voice, husky with tenderness, replied, 'You know I did.'

'Let's go or we'll miss the start of the movie. But you will find out what you can?'

'I'll take a run over there tonight.'

There was a scraping-back of chairs, then Agatha heard their retreating footsteps.

She felt desperately alone now. Bill's friendship had always been rock-solid. He had been her first friend in a hitherto friendless life. Now she felt she had no one to trust, certainly not James, who seemed to be handling the current situation by treating her as impersonally as he would another man.

And yet Bill Wong was obviously very much in love. What could he see in such a hard-faced bitch?

41

James looked at Agatha's gloomy face on her return and demanded to know what had upset her.

Wearily, Agatha told him of the overheard conversation.

James listened, his blue eyes intent. Then he said, 'You cannot blame Bill for falling in love with an ambitious woman detective. I don't think it'll last long. You can't choose his girlfriends for him.'

'When he calls this evening,' said Agatha huffily, 'I'm not speaking to him.'

'And what good will that do? He's our only contact with the police. Instead of going into a huff, Agatha, you should simply tell him what you overheard. Maddie said some nasty things about you, but Bill said none.'

'I don't want to speak to him again!'

'Agatha, be sensible.'

'I'm sick and tired of being sensible,' shouted Agatha and she burst into tears.

He gave her a clean handkerchief, he fetched her a stiff brandy, he suggested she lie down.

And Agatha, who had suddenly and desperately wanted a shoulder to cry on, a shoulder to lean on, pulled herself together and said on a sob that, yes, she would see Bill.

She would have been comforted could she have known that James felt as if he could cheerfully strangle both Bill Wong and Maddie, but James showed none of this as he returned to his computer. Agatha went up to bed for a nap; James tried to work, but his doorbell sounded shrilly. He thought it must be some persistent

42

member of the press. Normally he would not have answered the door, but he had a desire to relieve his feelings on somebody, even if that somebody was Bill Wong.

So he opened the door and found Roy Silver on the step.

James took the hapless Roy by the throat and shook him hard. 'Get the hell away from here, you little worm,' he roared. James gave him a final shake and then a push and Roy staggered backwards and fell into the hedge.

'I only came to help,' said Roy shrilly. 'Honest. I've got information about Jimmy Raisin. I've found out things which might explain why someone murdered him. I did it to help Aggie.'

James, who had been about to slam the door, hesitated. 'What are you talking about?'

Roy extricated himself from the hedge and tittuped forward cautiously. 'I hired a detective to find out about Jimmy Raisin. I've got her report.' He held up the briefcase he had managed to hang on to during James's assault on him.

'Oh, very well,' said James. 'Come in and I'll see if Agatha's prepared to listen to you.'

When Agatha came down the stairs, Roy backed nervously behind a chair. He had blonded his hair, which somehow made his face look weaker and whiter.

But Agatha had had time to think. If Roy had any worthwhile information, then she and James might solve the case and that would leave Bill and his precious Maddie with egg all over their faces.

'Sit down, Roy,' she said. 'If you've got anything of importance, I'd like to hear it, but don't think I'm ever going to forgive you for what you did to me.'

'He stopped you from committing bigamy,' said James.

Agatha glared at both of them.

'Let's hear what he has to say,' said James mildly.

Agatha nodded. Roy edged round the chair and sat down nervously, his briefcase on his lap. 'I assume,' said Agatha, 'that you initially hired this detective out of spite to find out if I was still married, and hired the detective again because you couldn't live with yourself, you creep!'

Roy cleared his throat. 'Always looking for the worst motives, aren't we, Aggie? I thought your husband was dead and I thought you would thank me if I gave you conclusive proof of that death as a wedding present. And you can huff and puff but that's the truth, or may God strike me dead!'

Agatha looked at the beamed ceiling. 'I'm waiting for the thunderbolt to fall on you, Roy.'

'This is getting us nowhere,' said James sharply. 'Let's hear your report.'

Roy opened the briefcase and took out a sheaf of papers.

'I wondered how it was that Jimmy had managed to live so long,' he said. 'But it seems that at one time a philanthropist, a Mrs Serena Gore-Appleton, had taken Jimmy up as a worthwhile cause and borne him off to

44

an expensive health farm. Although the place was hardly the Betty Ford Clinic and more a place where rich boozers went to dry out to recover and drink another day, it seemed to have worked for Jimmy, who became clean and sober and subsequently worked as a counsellor for Mrs Gore-Appleton's charity, Help Our Homeless. Now here's the interesting bit.

'Jimmy always seemed to have a lot of money to flash around. How my detective, a Ms Iris Harris, found that out was because Jimmy liked to queen it in front of his old down-and-out cronies. Then, after a year of sobriety, he suddenly went downhill amazingly quickly and soon reappeared among the beggars, junkies and general drop-outs of the London streets.

'One down-and-out who has recently sobered up offered the information that Jimmy delighted in finding out things about people, and even in his lowest stage was not above blackmailing someone for a bottle of meths with some threat such as reporting them to social security if he found out they had work and were still drawing the dole, that kind of thing.'

Roy beamed about him triumphantly. 'So you see, sweeties, this agile brain of mine came to the conclusion that if Jimmy could blackmail the poor, why not the rich while working with this Gore-Appleton female? Maybe he saw one of his pigeons in Mircester and the pigeon saw a likely opportunity of killing Jimmy and took it.'

'It all seems too much of a coincidence,' said James slowly. 'Agatha here decides to get married in Mircester.

45

Had it not been for that, Jimmy would never have come down to the Cotswolds. Why on earth should one of his victims suddenly appear as well?'

Roy looked downcast. Then his face brightened. 'Ah, but do you know where the health farm he went to is situated? At Ashton-le-Walls, ten miles outside Mircester.'

'Yes, but people who go to health farms don't usually come from the immediate neighbourhood, do they?' asked Agatha. 'I mean, they come from all over the country.'

'Oh, you are such a pair of *downers*!' said Roy petulantly. 'And coincidences do happen in real life. Do you remember that Australian friend of mine, Aggie? The tourist from hell?'

'Yes, I thought he was rather nice. Steve, that was his name.'

'Anyway, him. I thought he was back in Australia, never to return. The other week I was in a pub and I got talking about Steve to this friend, about his dreary camcorder and his dreary guidebooks, and I was just saying I hoped I would never see him again when I felt these eyes drilling into the back of my head and I turned round and there was Steve! He flounced off but I can tell you, it gave me a turn, and it was in a pub in Fulham I've never been to before.'

James turned to Agatha. 'He's at least given us something to go on. We should start off tomorrow by going up to London to try to find this Mrs Gore-Appleton.'

Agatha brightened visibly at the thought of taking some action.

The doorbell rang. 'That'll be Bill Wong,' said James, getting to his feet.

Agatha grabbed his sleeve. 'Let's not tell him anything about this, James. Let's keep it to ourselves for a bit.'

He looked about to protest and then slowly nodded. 'All right, but no getting yourself into danger again, Agatha. You've been involved in some scary murders in the past.'

Bill Wong came in and stopped short, surprised to see Roy.

'I thought they would have killed you.'

'Aggie and I are old friends,' said Roy defensively. 'I only wanted to give her Jimmy's death certificate as a wedding present.'

Bill gave him a slanting cynical look. 'If you say so.'

Roy picked up the papers, which James had left on the table, and thrust them into his briefcase.

'What's that?' asked Bill.

'PR stuff,' said Roy. 'I came down here to get Agatha's help.'

Bill looked around at the three faces. There was a wary, almost hostile atmosphere in the room. He decided ruefully that James and Agatha must be under a great strain. He should have called before this.

'I wish I had some good news for you,' he said, 'but we still cannot find out any reason why your late husband was murdered, Agatha. If it had been among the

47

down-and-outs in London, then it might have been decided he had been killed for no greater reason than the bottle in his pocket. But here, in the Cotswolds?'

'Haven't the police in London been questioning his old cronies?' asked James.

'Of course. But that lot have only to see a police uniform to clam up, and they can smell a detective at a hundred paces. I wish I could go there myself and see what I could dig up. How's the village taking it?' said Bill, who lived in Mircester.

'I gather Agatha and I are being regarded as first and second murderer,' said James. 'Tell us about the forensic evidence, Bill.'

'Pretty much still what I told Agatha. He had been strangled with a man's silk tie. Now that sounds like a good clue, but it is a Harvey Nichols tie and can be bought at just about any good outfitters in the country. It's also quite old and frayed at the edges.'

'That was Jimmy's own tie,' said Agatha suddenly. 'He wasn't wearing it when I last saw him but he had it on at the wedding. Wait a bit. Maybe he had it in his pocket. He wouldn't surely stand there and let someone fish in his pockets for a murder weapon?'

'What did the tie look like?' asked Bill. 'I can't remember.'

But Agatha did. She thought every horrible fact and item of that day would be burned into her brain forever. 'It was one of those ones which look like an old school tie but aren't – discreet stripes. Dark blue, gold and green.'

Bill whipped out a notebook and scribbled busily. Then he said, 'We've found out he got cleaned up in a Salvation Army hostel before he came down here and they gave him clothes. Of course, they probably gave him the tie as well.'

'Was he hit with anything first?' asked Agatha.

'Only the back of your hand.'

'He can't just have stood there and let it happen.'

'I think I know,' said Roy triumphantly. 'He's lying there in the ditch after Aggie here swiped him. Now, if you're a drunk and someone swipes you and you fall in the ditch, the first thing you'd do would be to take that bottle out of your pocket to make sure it hadn't got broken. Then you'd take a good swig out of it. Maybe when he pulled the bottle out of his pocket, the tie came out as well. Enter murderer. Jimmy in ditch, Jimmy with bottle to his mouth, tie sticking out of pocket, seizes tie, strangle, choke, one dead body.'

'Thank you, Mr Jingle,' said James. 'Mind you, it's possible. What do you think, Bill?'

'I think you all know something you aren't telling me,' said Bill, looking at them.

'How's dear Maddie?' asked Agatha sweetly.

His round face flushed. 'Detective Constable Hurd is well, thank you.'

'Do, please, please, give her my regards.'

Bill wondered in that moment whether Agatha had guessed that Maddie had sent him to find out what he could and then decided that love was making him paranoiac.

'I'd best be going.' Bill got to his feet.

'See you around,' said Agatha. James showed him out.

Bill stood outside the cottage for a moment, irresolute. He had not received his usual welcome. It was unlike both Agatha and James not to offer him a drink or a cup of coffee. He wondered for a moment whether he should go back and tell Agatha the truth, that he had not come near her before this because Maddie had urged him to do so. He took half a step back towards the door and then gave his round head an angry little shake and went towards his car instead.

So the three amateur detectives inside were free to start their investigations, unhampered by any help from the police.

50

Chapter Three

Agatha was silent on the drive to London the following morning. James, used to Agatha's holding forth on every subject under the sun, found this unnatural silence was making him uneasy. Furthermore, Agatha was wearing trousers and a sweater and no make-up and sensible walking shoes. No perfume either. He was obscurely piqued that for the first time Agatha should appear to make no effort whatsoever on his behalf.

The last known address for Help Our Homeless was in a basement in Ebury Street in Victoria. They had found it in James's very out-of-date set of London telephone directories. James wished they had tried to phone first, for it turned out to be now a minicab firm.

They found the boss of the minicab firm, a large West Indian, lounging back with his feet on the desk.

'We're looking for Help Our Homeless.'

'You an' everyone else, guv,' said the West Indian. 'Tell you what I told them. Don't know. Don't care.'

'Why is everyone else looking for them?' asked James.

'Same reason as what you are, guv. Money owing.'

'So you have no idea where Mrs Gore-Appleton is now?' asked Agatha.

'Search me.' He heaved his shoulders in a massive shrug, picked up a coffee cup, took a gulp of the contents and appeared to forget their very existence.

'Did you buy this place from her?' pursued James.

The man's dark eyes focused impatiently on them again. 'I bought it from Quickie Photocopying and Printing. Before that it was the Peter Pan Temp Agency, before that, Gawd knows. Nobody stays here long. Business rates are diabolical, trust me, guv. That Help Our Homeless died about four years ago.'

They gave up and left. James stood on the pavement head down, scowling furiously. 'If Help Our Homeless was a charity, then surely this Gore-Appleton must have been in the press, opening something, talking about something. Do you know a helpful reporter?'

'I used to know lots of journalists, but they were usually fashion editors or show-biz.'

'But they would have access to the records. Can we ask?'

Agatha searched her brain for a journalist she knew who might not hate her too much. When she had been a public relations officer, the press had regarded her as a pain in the neck and usually featured her clients just to get rid of her.

'I know the show-biz editor of *The Bugle*,' she said reluctantly. 'Mary Parrington.'

'Let's go and see her.'

They drove slowly down to the East End. Fleet Street was no more. The big papers had all relocated to cheaper, larger sites.

At last they stood in the sterile steel-and-glass hall of *The Bugle*, waiting to see whether Mary Parrington would grant them an audience.

Fortunately for Agatha, the news editor had been passing Mary's desk just as she was telling her secretary, 'Tell that awful old bat, Agatha Raisin, I'm dead or gone, or anything.'

'Wait a bit,' said the news editor. 'That's the female involved in the Cotswold murder. Get her up here and introduce me. No reporter's been able to get near her.'

The idea of throwing Agatha to the lions of the news desk greatly appealed to Mary, and so Agatha and James were shown up.

As he was introduced to the beaming news editor, a Mike Tarry, James reflected that he had accused Agatha of being naïve over the house sale, and yet he himself had walked straight into a newspaper office without pausing to think that he and Agatha were news themselves.

'Well, Agatha,' said Mike, after having practically strong-armed them into his office – 'I may call you Agatha?'

'No,' said Agatha sourly.

'Ha ha. Mary told me you were a tough character. How can we be of help? You must be anxious to clear your name.' The offices had windows overlooking the reporters' desks. Mike waved an arm. The door of his office opened and a photographer came in, followed by a reporter.

'What is this?' demanded Agatha.

'You help us and we'll help you,' said Mike.

'I'm off,' said Agatha, heading for the door.

'Wait a minute,' called James. Agatha turned back reluctantly.

'We do need help, Agatha,' said James, 'and we should have realized they would want a story. They've been pestering us since the murder. We've got nothing to hide. We want to find this Gore-Appleton woman. Why don't we just tell them what we know?'

'And then the police will wonder why we didn't tell *them* what we've found out,' pointed out Agatha.

'We would have told them sooner or later. May as well get it over with, Agatha. You're in the lions' den now, and even if you walk out, that photographer is going to bash off a picture of you before you get out of the office.'

'Let him,' said Agatha truculently.

'Agatha, you haven't any make-up on.'

And that clinched it.

The interviews and photographs had to wait until Agatha was ferried off to the shops by a 'minder' to buy make-up and a smart dress and high heels.

Then they both told what they knew, and Agatha and James posed for photographs, Agatha having extracted a promise that the art department would use the air-brush generously on her picture.

But when the reporter searched the files for details about Mrs Gore-Appleton, he found practically nothing, only one mention of her making a speech on the homeless at a charity event. No photograph. Agatha felt cheated until James pointed out that the publicity would be the one thing to flush out Mrs Gore-Appleton.

There seemed nothing left to do but allow themselves to be entertained to lunch, return to Carsely, and find out what the article in the following morning's paper would bring.

Agatha struggled awake the next morning out of a heavy sleep. Someone was banging on her bedroom door. She put on her dressing-gown and then stood, irresolute. The someone would be James, of course. The article must be in the paper. She debated whether to ask him to wait until she changed, but then shrugged. The days of dressing up for James had gone.

She opened the door. He was brandishing a copy of *The Bugle*. 'Would you believe it!' he raged. 'Not a bloody word!'

'Come down to the kitchen,' said Agatha. 'Are you sure you didn't miss it?'

'Not a word,' he repeated angrily.

Agatha sat down wearily at the kitchen table and spread out the newspaper. The headline screamed, FREDDIE COMES OUT OF THE CLOSET! A comedian, the pet of British audiences for his clean humour, had declared he was gay. The other story on page one was about a *Bugle* reporter who had been shot by the Bosnian Serbs.

'We never heard a word about these stories when we were in the office,' said Agatha. 'They must have broken in the afternoon and knocked our story out of the paper.'

'Maybe they'll run it tomorrow.'

Agatha shook her head, wise in the way of newspapers. 'They won't use it now,' she said gloomily. 'If they had had the story right at the time of the murder, they would have used it no matter what. But now it's sort of yesterday's news.'

'I'll phone up that editor and give him a piece of my mind.'

'Wouldn't do any good, James. We'll need to think of something else.'

He paced up and down the kitchen. 'I feel frustrated,' he said. 'I want to do something *now*.'

'That health farm,' said Agatha. 'The one Jimmy went to. We could go there and perhaps get a look at the records and see who was there at the same time, pick out the people Jimmy might have thought of blackmailing.'

James brightened. 'Good idea. What's the name of the place?'

'I've got Roy's notes in the living-room. Look there. They might be cagey about letting us see their records, so perhaps we'd best check into this health farm as guests and under false names.'

56

'We'll check in as man and wife. Mr and Mrs Perth, that'll do.'

James hurried off, leaving Agatha to marvel at the sheer insensitivity of men. Husband and wife, indeed, and without a blush!

Agatha went back upstairs to wash and dress. She longed to be in her own home again. Perhaps she should call on Mrs Hardy one more time.

Mrs Hardy answered the door to Agatha half an hour later. She was as muscular and tweedy as ever, and a truculent look lit up her eyes when she saw Agatha.

'Look,' said Agatha, 'I wondered if you would reconsider letting me have my cottage back. I would pay you a generous sum.'

'Oh, go away,' said Mrs Hardy. 'I am working to settle in here and could do without these tiresome interruptions from you. I hear you were once a businesswoman. Behave like one.'

She slammed the door in Agatha's face.

'Stupid old trout!' raged Agatha to James when she returned to join him and told him about Mrs Hardy's continued refusal to sell the house.

'Why bother?' said James. 'There are other houses, you know. I heard in the village that the Boggles are thinking of moving to an old folks' home. That means you could buy their house.'

Agatha gazed at him, aghast. 'But the Boggles live in a *council* house.'

'What's wrong with that? Some of these council houses are very well built. And the Boggles' place would be quite roomy once you got the junk out.'

Agatha wondered if he thought a council house was all she was good enough for and then considered in time that James did not know of her low beginnings and was merely being infuriatingly practical.

'Buy it yourself,' she muttered.

'I might at that. Get packed. I've booked us in at the health farm. It's called Hunters Fields. We're expected there this evening. I'll take Roy's notes with us. Don't look so miserable. Forget about your cottage for the moment. We'll think of something.'

'What? Snakes through the letterbox?'

'Something like that.'

Agatha went to call on Mrs Bloxby before they left. 'So you and James do seem to be getting on very well,' said the vicar's wife.

'The only reason we are getting on well is because James has all the sensitivity of a rhinoceros,' said Agatha drily. 'He's checking us into this health farm as man and wife.'

'Perhaps he is using that as an excuse for you to really get together again,' ventured Mrs Bloxby. She looked at Agatha's set face and added hurriedly, 'Perhaps not. He is a most unusual man. I think he keeps his mind in little compartments. The compartment of romantic Agatha

58

has the door firmly shut on it while the compartment with Agatha as friend is open. It's better than nothing, or is it agonizing?'

'Not really,' said Agatha. 'I find I can't think of him in the old way any more.'

'Because that would mean hurt?'

'Yes,' said Agatha gruffly and her small eyes filled with tears.

'I'll make some tea,' said Mrs Bloxby, tactfully going off and allowing Agatha time to recover.

'If only I could get my old cottage back,' mourned Agatha when Mrs Bloxby returned with the tea-tray. 'James is so well organized, I feel superfluous. I want my own things about me again.'

'I called on Mrs Hardy.' The vicar's wife carefully poured tea into two thin cups. 'She made a little speech about keeping herself to herself, that kind of thing. In fact, she was quite rude. Perhaps you should look for somewhere else?'

'I'll have to,' said Agatha. 'I'm embarrassed by the fact that so many people have refused to take their presents back, including you. I know you don't suspect us of the murder, but I suppose most people in the village do, and that is why they really don't want to have anything to do with us.'

'It's not quite that. Yes, lots of people did suspect you of the murder, but then good sense asserted itself and they became ashamed of themselves. The reason they do not want their presents back is because they think, because of the way you are both going on, that you and James will get married after all, and they do not want to be troubled by finding a suitable card and wrapping all over again.'

'Oh dear,' said Agatha harshly. 'Then they are doomed to disappointment.'

Mrs Bloxby changed the subject and regaled Agatha with some of the more innocent village gossip until Agatha finally took her leave.

Hunters Fields was a large mansion set in pretty parkland. When James told Agatha what they were charging, Agatha blinked in sheer horror. James insisted on paying the astronomical prices, saying he had recently been left a legacy by an aunt and was comfortably off.

They were shown to a spacious room on the first floor by a pretty receptionist who said the director would be with them shortly to explain the programme and the facilities of the centre.

The room had twin beds set well apart. They had just finished unpacking and hanging away their clothes when the director entered. He was a smooth-faced man with silver hair, well-tailored clothes, small gold-rimmed glasses and a benign air. He introduced himself as Mr Adder.

'The most important thing,' he said, 'is for our resident doctor to examine you both in the morning. We are careful about that. We do not like to subject our clients to too strenuous a programme if they are not up to it.' His eyes surveyed Agatha and James. 'You, Mr Perth, look too fit to need our help.'

'It was my wife's idea.'

'Ah, yes, I see.' The mild eyes turned on Agatha and she could feel those little rolls of fat at her middle-aged waist growing bigger.

Mr Adder went on to outline the facilities – massage, sauna, swimming pool, tennis courts, and so on.

James said, 'We would be interested to see your records.'

'Why?' A small frown now marred Mr Adder's normally bland face.

'An acquaintance of ours, a certain Jimmy Raisin, stayed here once. At the same time, some other people we might know might have been staying here and—'

'No, no, no, Mr Perth. Our records are confidential. Dinner is in half an hour.'

He departed after giving them an odd little bow.

'Well, that's that,' said Agatha gloomily.

'We'll just need to break into the office,' said James.

This he repeated after a minuscule dinner. 'I don't think I can bear to stay the whole week, Agatha,' he said.

'Oh, I don't know,' protested Agatha. 'Might be good for us.' Now that they were settled, she was looking forward to a trimming-down session.

'If I have to dine on this rabbit fodder for a whole week, my temper will become unbearable,' said James.

61

He looked around the other guests. They were mostly middle-aged and all looked rich.

'So when do you plan to break into the office?'

'Tonight,' said James. 'We'll take a look around after dinner. Wherever it is, it can't possibly be locked. A respectable place like this has no reason to suspect anyone would want to snoop.'

'We may have given Mr Adder reason to think we might. For all we know, he may have something pretty ordinary to hide, like one set of accounts for himself and one for the income tax.'

'Well, we'll see.' James sipped moodily at his decaffeinated coffee. 'And then, after we've located the office, we should drive to the nearest pub and get something to eat.'

Agatha wanted to protest. She felt slimmer already. But she knew it would irritate James if she insisted on dieting when she ought to be investigating.

After dinner, they walked around and found the office off the hall. It had a glass window which overlooked the hall, so they could clearly see filing cabinets and two computers. Not only was the office locked but so were the other rooms adjoining – sauna, massage room, treatment room, doctor's room and director's room.

'How are you going to open the door?' asked Agatha.

'I brought some lock-picks with me.' James had used a set of lock-picks before, never volunteering to explain why or how he had first got them.

They then drove down to a nearby village, where James ate a large helping of steak and kidney pie while Agatha contented herself with a ham sandwich and a glass of mineral water.

And then back to their room. James suggested they change into dark clothes, lie on top of their beds, and he would set the alarm for two in the morning.

Once in his bed, he fell asleep immediately while Agatha lay awake and listened to the gentle rumbling of her stomach. Just when she thought she would never fall asleep at all, she did, and then awoke with a start as the alarm sounded shrilly.

'Time to go,' said James. 'Let's hope they don't have some security guard patrolling the place to make sure the guests don't raid the kitchens.'

He opened the bedroom door. The corridor outside was brightly lit. He retreated back into the room. Agatha was wearing a navy sweater and black trousers and he was in a black sweater and black trousers. 'It's very bright out there,' he said, 'and we look like a couple of burglars. Do you think we should put on our dressing-gowns and then we can claim we were searching for food? They must be used to that.'

'They will wonder what we are doing searching for food in their files. Perhaps if we put something ordinary on. We both have jogging suits. We can say we were out for a run. We can say, if we're caught, that we are paranoiac about our private lives and wanted to see what was on file, something like that.'

'All right,' said James, starting to take off his trousers. Agatha felt obscurely miffed that he should undress so unselfconsciously in front of her.

She herself changed into a scarlet jogging jacket and trousers in the bathroom. She did not want James to see any of the middle-aged body he had rejected.

Her face looked wan in the fluorescent lights of the bathroom. Perhaps just a little foundation cream and a bit of powder. Maybe a bit of blusher. That new shade of red lipstick would go nicely with her jogging suit. She was just reaching for the mascara when James's impatient voice sounded from the other side of the bathroom door. 'What are you *doing*, Agatha? Are you going to be in there all night?'

'Coming.' Agatha regretfully abandoned the mascara and went out to join him. As she followed him out into the corridor, she realized again that the metabolism of Agatha Raisin did not thrive on health food. She was sure she had bad breath and her stomach was full of gas. She fell back behind James, cupped her hands and breathed into them, but James looked over his shoulder and demanded, 'What are you doing now?' and Agatha mumbled, 'Nothing,' fell into step beside him and prayed to all the gods who look after middle-aged ladies that she would not fart. The silence in the building was absolute.

They reached the hall without having met anyone or heard anyone.

When they reached the office, James murmured, 'It's a simple Yale lock. A plastic credit card might do it.' He took one out of his pocket and fiddled away while Agatha stood behind him, hearing the vague rumbles in her own stomach. Lights were blazing everywhere. She had brought a torch, but both the hall and the office were brightly lit. There was a click and James gave a grunt of satisfaction and opened the door.

'Where do we start?' whispered Agatha, looking at the computers. 'One of those?'

'They've got those old-fashioned filing cabinets. I bet the records about the time of Jimmy's visit are still in one of those.' He tried a top drawer of one. It slid open easily. 'Good,' he muttered. 'Let's hope there's something under Raisin.' He searched all the files in both cabinets without finding anything.

'Now what?' he asked.

'Try under Gore-Appleton,' urged Agatha. 'Jimmy could never afford a place like this, so it stands to reason she would make the booking and pay for it.'

He grunted and went back to his searching while Agatha stood looking through the office window into the hall in case anybody came.

At last he said, 'Got it! Gore-Appleton, 400a Charles Street, Mayfair. Booking for a Mr J. Raisin. Five years ago.'

Agatha groaned. 'But how do we find out who was resident at the same time?'

'Damn, I didn't think of that. We signed a book, a register. It was a fairly new one. The old ones must be somewhere.'

'What about that cupboard over there?'

'Locked,' said James. 'But simple to pick.'

Agatha waited while he fiddled with the lock, growing more nervous by the minute. Surely their luck could not continue to hold. And would she hear anyone coming? The whole place was thickly carpeted.

'Here we are,' said James. He took a small notebook out of his pocket and began to write.

'Hurry up,' pleaded Agatha.

'That's it,' he said after a few more agonizing minutes. 'Let's put it all back and lock up.'

Agatha heaved a sigh of relief when they were outside the office and back in the hall.

'What did you get?' she was asking when a smooth voice from the direction of the stairs made them both jump.

'Is there anything you need?' Mr Adder stood there in a black dressing-gown with a gold cord, his eyes gleaming behind his spectacles.

'No, no,' said James airily. 'Just been for a run.'

'Indeed,' said Mr Adder, approaching them, his eyes fastening on the notebook which James was shoving back into his pocket. 'How did you get outside? The doors are locked at midnight.'

'Up and down the stairs,' said Agatha.

'Up and down the *stairs*?'

'I am *so* silly,' gushed Agatha. 'I have these step things at home. You know, one of those exercise machines. Well, it's *vanity*. I really wanted to be trim and fit for my medical in the morning, so I said to James, "Let's run up and down the stairs." They are so thickly carpeted, I knew we wouldn't disturb anyone.'

Mr Adder's eyes were uncomfortably shrewd. 'You are therefore in better condition than I would have believed, Mrs Perth. You are not out of breath, neither are you sweating.'

'Oh, *thank you*!' said Agatha. 'I must really be quite fit, although I do confess to feeling a *teensy* bit tired. Bed, darling?'

'Good idea,' said James. 'See you in the morning, Mr Adder.'

He blocked their way. 'You must not try to run your own programme or this whole stay will be a waste of your money and our time. Do not wander about during the night.'

'Right,' said James, putting an arm around Agatha's shoulders. They walked on past Mr Adder.

Agatha looked back as they gained the stairs. Mr Adder was trying the office door to make sure it was locked.

'Phew,' she said, when they were back in their room. 'Think he swallowed that?'

'No, but he probably thought we were looking for the kitchens and tried the office door just to be sure. Now I chose the names out of the register of the people who live near Mircester who were here at the same time as Jimmy.' He flipped open the notebook. 'We have Sir Desmond Derrington and Lady Derrington, a Miss Janet Purvey and a Mrs Gloria Comfort. When we get out of here, however, the first thing we do is to go up to Charles Street in London and see if Mrs Gore-Appleton is still at the same address. Then we'll start on these names.'

'Have you paid for the whole week in advance?' asked Agatha.

'Yes.'

'So don't you think we should stay the whole week and get our money's worth?'

'I should die of boredom,' said James, turning away to pick up his pyjamas and so missing the look of naked hurt in Agatha's eyes. 'May as well both get our medical check-up, have a swim or a massage or something, and then get the hell out of here.'

Agatha found at her medical the following morning that her blood pressure and cholesterol levels were both a bit high. After a breakfast of muesli and fruit, she looked at her programme and went to the masseur to be pulled and pummelled, then a sauna and then to the gym for the morning's aerobics.

James was already there. The class was led by a blonde with long, long legs and a staggeringly beautiful figure. Agatha panted and sweated, aware the whole time that James's eyes were fastened on the vision leading the class. From wanting to stay on the whole week, she suddenly couldn't wait to get out of the place. After the class was over, she fidgeted impatiently while James chatted to the blonde instructress.

Over a meagre salad lunch and fruit juice, James looked at his own programme. 'Going easy on me for the first day,' he said. 'Not much this afternoon. Like to go for a swim?'

Agatha had a sudden mental picture of her own body set against the glory of that of the instructress. She shook her head. 'I thought we should be getting on with our investigations.'

'Right you are,' he said easily. 'But I thought you wanted to stay.'

'Mr Adder is over there and keeps darting little looks at us.'

'Agatha, I don't believe you. I think the aerobics class was too much for you.'

'Not in the slightest. I got a little puffed, that's all.'

'I wouldn't worry about Adder. It's quite pleasant here.' He laughed at the baffled look on Agatha's face. 'It's all right. We'll go. What excuse shall we give?'

'I have these fads. I'm a temperamental lady. I've changed my mind.'

'That should do the trick. If you've finished, go and start packing and I'll deal with Mr Adder.'

Dealing with Mr Adder proved trickier than James had expected. He listened in silence to James's tale of a temperamental wife, and then said, 'We don't give refunds.'

'I didn't suppose for a minute you did,' said James airily.

Mr Adder leaned forward. 'Have you heard of co-dependency therapy?'

'I beg your pardon?'

'I think you could do with some counselling, Mr Perth. We like to supply our customers with the best of service, and that includes looking after their mental welfare as well as their physical well-being. You appear to be in prime condition and yet you are married to a lady who gets you up in the middle of the night to run up and down the stairs. It strikes me that you have agreed to her whim to leave without protest. *You have been taken hostage, Mr Perth.*'

'Oh, Agatha and I get on all right.'

Mr Adder leaned forward and tapped James on the knee. 'Provided you always do exactly what she wants, hey?'

James put a shifty look on his face. 'Well, it's her money, you see.'

'And you go along with everything she wants because she holds the purse-strings?'

'Why not?' demanded James. 'I'm not getting any younger. Don't want to go out and look for work at my age.'

A look of distaste crossed Mr Adder's features. 'If you choose to earn your money being at your wife's beck and call, then there is nothing I can do for you. But I have never come across a man whose appearance was

70

more deceptive. I would have judged you a strong character of high morals and firm convictions who could not be bullied by anyone.'

'I am beginning to find you a trifle impertinent, Mr Adder.'

'Forgive me. I was only trying to help.'

James rose and escaped upstairs, where he told Agatha, with a certain amount of relish, that he was now regarded as a sponger of the first order who was bullied by his wife.

To Agatha's high irritation, the blonde beauty who led the aerobics class came out to say goodbye to James. Agatha waited angrily in the car, wondering what they were talking about. She saw James take out his notebook and write something down. Her phone number? Agatha's jealousy flared up. James was no longer hers and therefore prey to every blonde harpy who wanted to get her painted claws into him. By the time James finished his conversation, Agatha was feeling quite weepy.

At last James climbed into the driving seat. 'What was that all about?' asked Agatha, trying to keep her voice light.

'Oh, chit-chat,' he said. 'I think we should head straight for London to that address in Charles Street.'

The journey was completed in almost total silence, Agatha wrestling with a jumble of unwanted emotions and James immersed in his own thoughts.

At Charles Street, off Berkeley Square, they drew a blank. No Mrs Gore-Appleton had ever lived there.

'Didn't she pay by cheque or credit card?' asked Agatha.

'No, cash. It was on the records.'

'Damn. Now what?'

'Back to Carsely for the night. Then we'll try Sir Desmond Derrington tomorrow.'

Agatha could not sleep that night. She was determined to find out what James had written down in his notebook while he had been talking to the aerobics woman.

She waited until she was sure that James was asleep and then crept along to his room. It was brightly lit by moonlight and she could see his trousers hanging over the back of a chair, with the edge of the notebook sticking out of the back pocket.

Keeping a cautious eye on the sleeping figure on the bed, Agatha gently eased the notebook out and carried it back through to her room. She flicked it open and turned to the last entry. In James's cramped handwriting, which the eyes of love had taught her to decipher, 'Co-Dependency Anonymous', Agatha read with amazement. There followed a London address and a 'contact' number.

The bitch, thought Agatha, forgetting for the moment that she was supposed to be a fickle and domineering woman whose husband was dependent on her cash.

72

'So now you've satisfied your curiosity, madam, do you think I could have my notebook back?' James's voice rang from the doorway.

Agatha flushed guiltily. 'I was only looking at those names you found in the office.'

'Wrong page,' he said. 'You're supposed to be a bullying rich woman and I'm supposed to be a wimp of a leech, remember? Hence the therapy suggestion.'

'I thought you were asleep,' was all Agatha could think of saying.

'I wake easily, as you should know.'

'Sorry, James,' mumbled Agatha. 'Go back to bed.'

Chapter Four

Sir Desmond Derrington lived in a pleasant Cotswold mansion a few miles outside Mircester on the Oxford road. As they approached it, Agatha saw a poster stuck on a tree-trunk beside the road which advertised the fact that Sir Desmond's gardens were open that day to the public.

'I hope he's there,' said James when it was pointed out to him. 'I hope he hasn't gone off and left the local village ladies to show people around.'

Agatha, desperate for anyone who looked like a murderer, felt disappointed when she first saw Sir Desmond. He was bending over an ornamental shrub and explaining its history and planting to a fat woman who was shifting her bulk uneasily and looking as if she wished she had never asked about it. Sir Desmond looked like a pillar of the community, middle-aged, greying, long-nosed, and married to a rangy loud-voiced wife who was holding forth in another part of the garden. Lady Derrington was wearing a short-sleeved cotton print dress despite the chill of the day and had a hard flat

74

bottom and a hard flat chest. Her brown hair was rigidly permed and her patrician nose looked down at each flower and plant with a faintly patronizing air, as if all had sprung from the earth without her permission.

The fat woman waddled away from Sir Desmond and James approached him. 'I was admiring that fine wisteria you've got on the wall over there,' he said.

'Oh, that.' Sir Desmond blinked myopically in the direction of the house wall. 'Very fine in the spring. Masses of blossom.'

'I'm experiencing a bit of difficulty with mine,' said James. 'I planted it two years ago but it hasn't grown very much and has very few blossoms.'

'Where did you get it from?'

'Brakeham's Nurseries.'

'Them!' Sir Desmond gave a contemptuous snort. 'Wouldn't get anything from there. Hetty, my wife, got given a present of a hydrangea from there. Died after a week. And do you know why?' Sir Desmond poked James in the chest with a long finger. '*No roots.*'

'How awful. I'll give them a clear berth in future.'

Agatha was approaching to join them. Then she heard Sir Desmond say, 'Lot of charlatans about. Where are you from?'

'Carsely.'

'Do you know I went to see the gardens there when they were open to the public and some woman had bought everything *fully grown* from a nursery and tried

75

to pretend she had planted the lot from seed. Didn't even know the names of anything.'

Recognizing a description of herself, Agatha veered off, leaving the conversation to James.

She approached Lady Derrington instead. 'Nice garden,' said Agatha.

'Thank you,' said Lady Derrington. 'We have some plants for sale on tables over by the house. Very reasonable prices. And there are tea and cakes. Our housekeeper makes very good cakes. Just follow the crowd. Why, Angela, darling, how wonderful to see you!'

She turned away. Agatha looked back at James. He was now deep in conversation with Sir Desmond. Judging that they had moved from the subject of that dreadful woman in Carsely, Agatha went to join them. They were swapping army stories. Agatha fidgeted and stifled a yawn.

'I was just about to take a break and have some tea,' said Sir Desmond finally. 'Do join us. The women from the village are quite capable of coping with this crowd.'

James introduced Agatha as his wife, Mrs Perth. Agatha was surprised that he should maintain that bit of deception, but James did not want Sir Desmond to remember Agatha as the gardening cheat of Carsely.

Sir Desmond walked them over to his wife and introduced them. Lady Derrington seemed slightly displeased that two strangers should have been invited for tea. Agatha suspected that she would have been better pleased if they had paid for it.

76

They found themselves in a pleasant drawing-room. The green leaves of the wisteria fluttered and moved outside the windows, dappling the room in a mixture of sunlight and shadow. Two sleepy dogs rose at their entrance and yawned and stretched before curling down and going to sleep again. Lady Derrington threw a log on the fire and then poured tea. No cakes, noticed Agatha with a beady eye. Only some rather hard biscuits. She wanted a cigarette but there was no ashtray in sight.

They answered questions about Carsely and then James leaned back in his chair, stretched his long legs, and said with seeming casualness, 'My wife and I have just returned from a short stay at Hunters Fields.'

Sir Desmond was lifting a cup of tea to his lips. His hand holding the cup paused in mid-air. 'What's that?' he demanded sharply.

'It's that health farm,' said his wife. 'Horribly pricey. The Pomfrets went there but they've got money to burn.'

'But you were there yourself,' said James. 'You were both there at the same time as two people we know, Mrs Gore-Appleton and Jimmy Raisin.'

'We have never been there and I have never heard of them,' said Sir Desmond evenly. 'Now if you will forgive me . . .'

He stood up and walked to the door and held it open. His wife looked surprised but did not say anything.

He strode out angrily back into the gardens followed

by Agatha and James and then turned to face them. 'I'm tired of scum like you. You are not getting a penny.'

He rushed off, cannoned off a pair of surprised visitors, and disappeared around a corner of the house.

Agatha made to go after him but James held her back. 'He must have been there with someone else, someone who wasn't his wife. Leave it, Agatha. Someone was blackmailing him, probably Jimmy. It's time to tell Bill Wong what we know.'

They left a message for Bill Wong when they returned home, but it was the following day before they saw him again.

He arrived in the afternoon. When she opened the door, Agatha could see the dreadful Maddie sitting in the car. Bill followed Agatha into the living-room. 'Coffee?' said James.

'No, thank you. I haven't much time. What did you want to see me about?'

They told him about their investigations, ending up with the visit to Sir Desmond Derrington.

Bill Wong's chubby face was severe. 'I've been there all night,' he said sternly. 'Sir Desmond is dead. It *appears* to have been a shooting accident. His shotgun went off when he was cleaning it. But he was cleaning it in the middle of the night, you see, and it now seems to me he thought you were taking over where Jimmy Raisin left off. We roused the health farm at two in the morning. Sir

Desmond stayed there at the same time as Jimmy Raisin with a woman who gave her name as Lady Derrington. The real Lady Derrington is the one with all the money. Had she divorced Sir Desmond, he would have been virtually penniless. He had been paying out the sum of five hundred pounds a month for a year, probably the year Jimmy Raisin was sober, and then the payments stopped. He was proud of his position in the community – local magistrate, all that sort of thing. Does it dawn on you interfering pair that you might have killed him?'

'Oh, no,' said James, horrified. 'Surely it was an accident?'

'Why decide to clean a gun in the middle of the night, and the night after your visit?' said Bill wearily. 'It's dangerous to interfere with police work.'

James glanced sideways at Agatha's stricken face. 'Look,' he said, 'we were about to give you all this information anyway. So what would happen? You would start with the health farm and then you would call on Sir Desmond. Would you think of asking them to describe the woman who said she was Lady Derrington? No, you would not. So you would have approached him and he would know his wife was going to find out all about it and the result would have been the same.'

'We thought of that. But Maddie pointed out that a visit from the police might not have tipped the balance of his mind the way the appearance on the scene of what appeared to be a couple of blackmailers has done.'

'Maddie says, Maddie says,' jeered Agatha tearfully. 'You think the sun shines out of her arse!'

There was a shocked silence. Agatha turned red.

'Go upstairs and put some make-up on or something,' said James quietly. When Agatha had left the room, he said to Bill, 'Agatha heard an unfortunate conversation between you and Maddie in the pub in Mircester. The toilets are behind where you were both talking. Maddie was manipulating you into calling on us to find out if we knew anything. I gather her remarks about Agatha were pretty insulting. Had Agatha not been so badly hurt and had I not sympathized with her, we might have told you all this earlier. Friendship,' said James sententiously, 'is a valuable thing. All you had to say to Maddie was that you would be calling on us anyway as part of your investigations. Do you not feel she is using you to find out extra facts which might help *her* to solve the case?'

'No,' said Bill hotly. 'Not a bit of it. She is a hard-working and conscientious detective.'

'Oh, really? Well, let's return to the question of Sir Desmond's death. His wife held the purse-strings. So how did he manage to pay out this five hundred a month, if that was blackmail money and not some money to a young mistress, without his wife finding out?'

'He had a monthly income from Lady Derrington's family trust. It was generous, but Sir Desmond had quite an extravagant life-style in a quiet way. Hunting, for example, takes a bit of money, not to mention the shirts from Jermyn Street and the suits from Savile Row. Lady Derrington never checked his bank account. It was over-drawn each month. That came as a surprise to her.'

'So I gather you insensitive cops put her wise to the mistress. How did Lady Derrington take it?'

'Coldly. She said, "Silly old goat."'

'And who was this charmer who seduced Sir Desmond?'

'A secretary from the House of Commons, secretary to an MP friend of Sir Desmond's. We're trying to get her. She's on holiday in Barbados at the moment. Called Helen Warwick. Not young. Blonde, yes, but in her forties.'

'Married?'

'No.'

'So no blackmail there?'

'We'll need to wait and see. She is a respectable lady and might not want to feature in a divorce case. Look, I'd better talk to Agatha. Things overheard are always worse than things said direct.'

'Leave it for the moment,' said James curtly. 'I'll speak to her.'

'Well, don't do any more detecting without telling me. In fact, don't do any detecting at all.'

Bill left and climbed into the car beside Maddie. 'Well, did you tell that interfering pair what you thought of them?' she asked.

'I was the one that was made to feel guilty. Agatha overheard a conversation between us in the pub where you were urging me to sound them out to see what they knew and she also heard some of your unflattering remarks.'

'Serves her right.' Maddie shrugged.

For the first time, Bill's mind made a separation between lust and love. For a brief moment, he wondered if he even liked Maddie, but when she crossed her legs in their sheer black stockings, lust took over and rationalized all his feelings back into romance.

Agatha came back into the living-room and said in a weary voice, 'Has he gone?'

'Yes, and very guilty about having hurt you, too.' James surveyed Agatha. Her face was scrubbed free of make-up and she was wearing an old sweater and a rather baggy skirt and flat heels. He had always considered privately that women did not need to plaster their faces with make-up, but he found himself missing the Agatha of the high heels, make-up, French perfume and ten-denier stockings. He had not forgiven her for having made such a fool of him on the wedding day. Somewhere in his heart he knew he would never forgive her and therefore he did not want to get romantically involved with her again, but he did not like to see her so down and crushed.

'Bill has asked us to butt out, as usual,' said James, 'but I say, let's go on with it. That'll cheer you up. We'll

82

have an easy day and then try the next on the list, Miss Janet Purvey.'

'And have *her* kill herself?'

'Now, Agatha. Sir Desmond would have been found out anyway and the result would have been the same. Do you want to go out for dinner tonight?'

'I'll see. I promised to go to Ancombe with the Carsely Ladies' Society. We're being hosted by them. They're putting on a revue.'

'Well, well, the delights of the countryside. Have fun.'

'At the Ancombe Ladies' Society? You must be joking.'

'Why go?'

'Mrs Bloxby expects me to go.'

'Oh, in that case . . .'

Agatha was not religious. Often she thought she did not believe in God at all. But she was superstitious and felt obscurely that divine punishment for the death of Sir Desmond was just beginning when Mrs Bloxby asked her apologetically if she would mind taking the Boggles over to Ancombe in her car.

'I know, Agatha,' said Mrs Bloxby ruefully, 'but we put names in a hat before you came and you got the Boggles. Ancombe isn't far, about five minutes' drive at the most.'

'Okay,' said Agatha gloomily.

She drove round to the Boggles' home, named Culloden, on the council estate. Like most of the people on the estate, they had bought their house. How could James even think for a moment I would live in a place like this, thought Agatha. It was admittedly a well-built stone house, but exactly the same as all the other houses round about. She stood looking dismally up at it. The door opened and the squat figure of Mrs Boggle appeared, followed by her husband. 'Are you goin' to stand there all day,' grumbled Mrs Boggle, 'or are you coming to help me?'

Agatha repressed a sigh and went forward to support the bulk of Mrs Boggle, who smelt strongly of chips and lavender, towards the car.

They both got in the back while Agatha, chauffeur-like, got into the driving seat. Mrs Boggle poked Agatha in the back as she was about to drive off. 'Us shouldn't be going with the likes of you,' she said. 'Poor Mr Lacey. What a disgrace.'

Agatha swung round, her face flaming. 'Shut up, you old trout,' she said viciously. 'Or walk.'

'I'll tell Mrs Bloxby on you,' muttered Mrs Boggle but then relapsed into silence during the drive to Ancombe.

Agatha hoisted the two Boggles from the car outside Ancombe church hall and sent them inside and then went to join Mrs Mason, the chairwoman of the Carsely group, Miss Simms, the secretary, and Mrs Bloxby. 'Shame about you landing them Boggles,' said Miss Simms, Carsely's unmarried mother. 'Don't worry, I had them last time.'

'I didn't know you had a car,' said Agatha.

'My gentleman friend bought me one. Hardly the wages o' sin. Not a Porsche but a rusty old Renault 5.'

Agatha turned to Mrs Bloxby. 'Has that woman who's bought my cottage joined the Ladies' Society?'

'I did ask her,' said the vicar's wife, 'but she said she couldn't be bothered and shut the door in my face.'

'Nasty cow,' said Agatha. 'Oh, if only I hadn't sold my cottage! I'd better look for somewhere else. I can't live out of a suitcase at James's forever.' She walked off into the hall.

'Now there's a thing,' said Miss Simms, picking a piece of tobacco off her teeth. 'I thought the wedding would happen sooner or later.'

Doris Simpson, Agatha's cleaner, joined them. 'Poor Agatha,' she said. 'She do miss her home and I miss the cleaning.'

'Don't you do it for Mr Lacey, then?' asked Miss Simms.

'No, he does his own cleaning, and that's unnatural in a man, if you ask me.'

'I had a fellow like that once. Went off and left me for another fellow,' said Miss Simms. 'It all goes to show.'

'I do not think our Mr Lacey is that way inclined,' said Mrs Bloxby.

'Never can tell. Some of 'em don't come out o' the closet till they're quite old and then they run around saying, "This is the life," and bugger the wife and kids,' Mrs Simpson said.

'"Bugger" being the word,' said Miss Simms and she gave a cackle of laughter.

'Shall we go in, ladies?' suggested the vicar's wife.

The revue consisted of songs and sketches. In the way of amateur productions, the singer most on stage was the one with the weakest voice and had chosen to sing a selection from the musicals of Andrew Lloyd Webber, petering out in the high notes and dying in the low notes and shrill in the middle. The rendering of 'Don't Cry for Me Argentina' was, Agatha reflected sourly, music to stun pigs by.

Usually when she was out at some event that bored her, she looked forward to returning home to her cottage and cats. But there was only James's cottage to return to, where she seemed to exist by sufferance on the periphery of his well-ordered life.

Damn that Hardy woman, she thought. And then she stifled a little gasp. Mrs Hardy, that could be it! Come from God knows where. Who knew anything about her? And her arrival in the village had been coincidental with the death of Jimmy Raisin. Agatha barely heard the rest of the concert. She wanted to rush home and tell James about her suspicions, but there was tea to take afterwards and the grumbling Boggles to run home.

By the time she was free, her splendid idea had been replaced by doubts. But none the less she told James of her suspicions. To her relief, he listened to her seriously and said, 'I've been wondering about that woman myself. There doesn't seem much point in trying to talk to her; she doesn't seem the chatty sort, to say the least.'

There was a ring at the doorbell and Agatha went to answer it. Mrs Bloxby stood there. 'Come in,' said Agatha.

'I can't. I brought your scarf. You left it at the hall. I'm just going to pick up the keys from Mrs Hardy. For some reason she wants me to keep the spares while she's in London. I told her to leave them with our policeman, Fred Griggs, but she said she didn't want to.'

'When does she leave?' asked Agatha.

'About now, I think. I had better go.'

Agatha thanked her for the scarf and went thoughtfully back indoors.

'There's a thing,' she said, sitting down opposite James. 'The Hardy woman's off to London. Left her spare keys with Mrs Bloxby. Wouldn't it be interesting to get a look in there?'

'Can't very well ask Mrs Bloxby for the keys. And I wouldn't like to try lock-picking in broad daylight.'

'But I've got another set to the cottage. I found them in my case.'

'Won't she have changed the locks?'

'I've a feeling that one would not go to any expense if she could do otherwise. Oh, just think, James, what if she proves to be Mrs Gore-Appleton?'

'Too much to hope for. But I'd like to find out more about her. How do we get in there without anyone seeing us? There always seems to be someone about in this village when you don't want them to be, and we can't wait until the middle of the night. Did Mrs Bloxby say anything about when she planned to return?'

'No. But I have the key to the back door. All we need to do is go out and over the fence of your garden and then over the fence and into mine – I mean hers.'

'Okay. I'll go outside and weed the front garden so I can see her leaving.'

James, bent double over a flowerbed, thought after half an hour that Mrs Hardy might have changed her mind, but then, as he straightened up, he was rewarded by the sight of her truculent face behind the wheel of her car, heading off down Lilac Lane. He stood and craned his neck, hearing the sound of the car retreating through the village, and then seeing it climbing up the hill out of Carsely.

He went back indoors. 'Right, Agatha,' he said. 'Let's go.'

Agatha shinned over James's garden fence, thinking that detective work might prove too energetic a business for a middle-aged woman. James had gone over lightly and had crossed the narrow alley between his garden and that of Mrs Hardy and was already climbing over her fence.

That James should expect her to scramble after him without an offer of help riled Agatha. She felt she was being treated like a man. She suddenly wanted James to notice her again, really look at her as a man ought to look at a woman. She thought that when she reached the top of Mrs Hardy's fence, she would call to him for help. He would stretch his arms up to her and she would drop down into them, her eyes closed, and she would whisper, 'James, oh James.'

'Help!' she called softly. She dropped down the other side of the fence, stumbled and landed face-down in a flowerbed. She got to her feet and glared. James, totally oblivious to the romantic script she had written for him, was unlocking the kitchen door. Agatha gave herself a mental shaking. She did not love him any more, she told herself. It was just that she had become so used to being in love, to having her brain filled with bright dreams, that without them she was left with herself. Agatha did not find herself very good company.

She looked around her garden as she headed for the back door. It had a weedy, neglected air.

Inside the house, she looked around the kitchen. It was gleaming and sterile. She opened the fridge. Nothing but a bottle of milk and some butter. She was about to open the freezer compartment when James said angrily from behind her, 'We're not here to find out what she eats but who she is.'

She followed him through to the living-room. Agatha had never credited herself with having much taste, but looking around what had once been her cosy, chintzy living-room, she felt *her* cottage had undergone a species of rape. There was a mushroom-coloured fitted carpet on the floor. A three-piece suite in mushroom velvet was ornamented with gold tassels on the arms and gold fringe above the squat legs. A low glass coffee table glittered coldly. No pictures or books. Her lovely open hearth had been blocked up and an electric fire with fake logs stood in front of it.

'Absolutely nothing here,' said James. 'Let's try upstairs. You'd best stay down here in case you hear her coming back.' And Agatha was glad to agree, not wanting to see what Mrs Hardy had done to the rest of the cottage. She went to the window and peered out. Autumn had come. A thin mist was curling around the branches of the lilac bush at the gate. Water dripped from the thatch with a mournful sound.

Agatha suddenly wondered what on earth she was doing living in the country, a feeling that only assailed her during the autumn. It was the Cotswold fogs that were the problem. Last winter hadn't been too bad, but the winter before had been awful, crawling into Moreton-in-Marsh or Evesham to do the shopping with the fog-lights on, sometimes not knowing whether she was still on the road or not, driving home at night when the fog seemed to rear up and take on tall, pillared, shifting shapes, eyes aching, longing for the wind to blow and lift it.

In London there were shops, brightly lit, and tubes and buses, theatres and cinemas. Of course, she could get all that in Oxford, but Oxford was thirty miles away, thirty miles of fog-filled road.

She heard James call softly, 'You'd better come up here.'

She ran up the stairs. 'In here,' he called. 'The main bedroom.'

The room was dominated with a large four-poster bed, a modern four-poster bed. 'How did she get that up the stairs?' marvelled Agatha.

'Never mind. Look at this. Don't touch anything. I'm going to put it all back the way I found it.' There were papers spread out on the floor. Agatha knelt down and studied them. Any hope Agatha might have had that the mysterious Mrs Hardy might turn out to be the missing Mrs Gore-Appleton quickly fled.

There was a birth certificate: Mary Bexley, born in Sheffield in 1941. Then marriage lines. Mary Bexley had married one John Hardy in 1965. Death certificate for John Hardy. Died in car crash 1985.

Bank-books and statements in the name of Mary Hardy. There were photographs, dull and boring. It appeared that the late Mr Hardy had been the company director of an electronics firm. Photos of Mr Hardy at firm functions. No children.

'So that's very much that,' commented Agatha gloomily as she straightened up. James carefully replaced everything.

'We'll try Miss Janet Purvey tomorrow,' he said.

* * *

91

Miss Janet Purvey lived in Ashton-le-Walls, quite near the health farm. It was a sleepy village wreathed in the thick mist which still persisted to haunt the countryside. Late roses drooped over cottage walls, blackened busy Lizzies, suffering from the first frost of the autumn, drooped along the edge of flowerbeds. The trees were turning russet and birds piped dismally, seemingly the only sounds in the village of Ashton-le-Walls, where nothing and no one but Agatha and James seemed to be alive in the fog.

The year was dying and Agatha felt lost and strange and loveless. The only thing that seemed to be keeping her and James locked together was this detective investigation. She felt that once it was all over, they would drift apart, farther than they had ever been before, as if they had never lain in each other's arms.

A poem she had learned at school suddenly ran through Agatha's brain:

> *Western wind, when wilt thou blow?*
> *The small rain down can rain, –*
> *Christ, if my love were in my arms*
> *And I in my bed again!*

She felt if only the wind would blow away the mist and fog, her spirits would lighten. Autumn seemed to be inside her very brain, darkness and falling leaves and the haunting spectre of decay and old age.

Miss Purvey lived in a cottage called The Pear Tree in

the middle of the village. It was in a terrace of other small cottages, dark, secret and lightless in the fog.

Agatha had not asked James whether he knew how old this Miss Purvey was and dreaded finding out she was a sophisticated blonde who might capture James's affections.

Her first feeling on seeing Miss Purvey when she answered the door was one of relief, the second, contempt accompanied by the thought, what a frumpy old bag.

The middle-aged, like Agatha, can be extremely cruel about the old, possibly because they are looking at their immediate future. Miss Purvey was, in fact, only about seventy, with a mouth like Popeye, a small nose, twinkling watery eyes and rigidly permed white hair. Her face was wrinkled and sallow. Only in Britain, thought Agatha, looking at the sunken line of the jaw and the thin, drooping mouth, could you still come across women of means who went in for having their teeth removed. It was still George Orwell's country of people with bad teeth or no teeth at all.

'No reporters,' said Miss Purvey in a plummy voice.

'We are not reporters,' said James. 'Have you had the press here?'

'No, but the police have been asking me impertinent questions. Are you Jehovah's?'

'No, we're—'

'Selling something?'

'No,' said James patiently.

93

'Then what?' The door began to inch closed.

'I am Mrs Agatha Raisin,' said Agatha, stepping in front of James.

'The widow of that man who was murdered?'

'Yes.'

'Well, I'm very sorry for you, but I can't help you.'

James took over. 'I feel perhaps you can, Miss Purvey. You look like a charming and intelligent woman to me.' He smiled and Miss Purvey suddenly smiled back. 'We are concerned to find out what Mrs Raisin's husband was doing at the health farm. We need a *lady* with good powers of observation rather than some dry police report.'

'Well . . .' She hesitated. 'Mother always used to say I noticed what the average person missed. Do come in.'

Agatha followed James into the cottage quickly, feeling that Miss Purvey would have been quite happy to shut the door in her face.

The cottage was as dark as the day outside. A small fire burned in the living-room grate. There were photographs everywhere, on the many side tables, on the upright piano in the corner, and on the mantelpiece, old photographs taken on forgotten sunny days.

'So,' began James when they were seated, 'did you speak to Mr Raisin?'

'Only a little,' said Miss Purvey. 'And to be quite frank, I was amazed that such a type of person should be at such an expensive health farm.'

94

'But you saw him,' said James. 'What was your impression of him?'

She put her finger to her forehead, rather like the Dodo in *Alice*, and frowned. 'He was very friendly to everyone, chatting here and there and table-hopping at meals. He had a very loud laugh. His clothes were good, but they didn't seem to belong to him. Not a gentleman.'

'And Mrs Gore-Appleton?'

'She seemed quite all right. But too old to have her hair dyed that improbable shade of gold and her exercise clothes were much too flashy.'

'Was she in love with Mr Raisin?' asked James.

'They were very much a couple and I saw him going into her room in the middle of the night.' Miss Purvey's lips folded in such disapproval that they disappeared into the lines of her face.

'But you personally did not have anything to do with him?' Agatha put in.

'He did ... er ... *come on to me*. That is the modern expression, is it not? But I would have none of it.'

Both Agatha and James were struck by the same thought at the same time, that it was hard to imagine Miss Purvey repulsing the advances of any man. There was an avid eagerness about her as she looked at James and she constantly reached out to touch his arm. 'But then,' she went on, 'he turned his attentions to Lady Derrington, or the woman who, I now gather, was not Lady Derrington. I fear these health clinics nurture *lax morals*.'

'Did the police broach the subject of blackmail with you?' asked James.

'Yes, they did. But as I pointed out, there are still *ladies* around in these days.' Miss Purvey's eyes rested briefly on Agatha, as if dismissing her from the lady class.

'Can you think of anyone he might have been blackmailing?' Agatha's voice was thin with dislike.

'I don't know if he was blackmailing her. But there was a certain Mrs Gloria Comfort. He was all over her. Mrs Gore-Appleton didn't seem to mind.'

'What was Mrs Gore-Appleton really like?' asked Agatha. 'I don't mean her appearance, but her character.'

'Well, as I said, she was a lady,' said Miss Purvey reluctantly. Again those eyes fastened on Agatha. 'And although her clothes were unsuitable, they were very expensive. She was well made-up and quite thin, but very fit.' So goodbye, Mrs Hardy, thought Agatha, conjuring up a picture of that powerfully built woman. Agatha still nourished hopes that Mrs Hardy would miraculously turn out to be the missing Mrs Gore-Appleton, but then she desperately wanted her cottage back.

Agatha began to fidget. She now loathed Miss Purvey and felt the small dark living-room claustrophobic.

But James seemed determined to discuss the matter further, and to Agatha's dismay accepted an offer of coffee. He followed Miss Purvey into the kitchen to help her. Agatha walked around the room looking at the photographs. They all featured Miss Purvey at various stages of her life. Agatha was surprised to note that as a young woman she had been very pretty. Why hadn't she married? There were parents and what looked like two brothers. There was a photo of Miss Purvey at her coming-out in the days when debs were still presented at court, so the family must have had money. She could hear the voices from the kitchen and then heard Miss Purvey give a flirtatious laugh. Damn James!

They returned from the kitchen together, Miss Purvey's old face slightly pink. To Agatha's amazement, Miss Purvey's attitude to her had changed. She pressed Agatha to try her cakes and then chatted about life in the village and the work she was doing for the Women's Institute. 'Ladies like us, Mrs Raisin,' she said, 'must do our bit.'

'Yes,' agreed Agatha faintly, wondering what had brought about this change and not knowing that James had whispered to Miss Purvey the lie that Agatha was a niece of the Duke of Devonshire.

'Now although I said Mrs Gore-Appleton was a lady,' confided Miss Purvey, putting a wrinkled hand on Agatha's knee, 'I did get the impression that she had gone to the bad, if you know what I mean. It's hard to put my finger on it, but there was a raffishness about her, a seediness, and something else . . . I don't know what, but I was quite frightened of her. As I was telling Mr Lacey, I remember she did begin to talk to me towards the end of my stay. She was talking about money and business and told me she was running a charity. She said that everyone had money worries today and I said I was quite comfortably off, thank you, and she asked me if I would contribute to her charity, but when I heard it was for the homeless, I refused. I said if these people were homeless, then it was their own fault.'

To Agatha's relief, James abruptly lost interest in anything further that Miss Purvey might have to say. He put down his cup.

'Thank you for your hospitality. We really must be going.'

'Oh, must you? I could be of help to you, I think.'

'You have already been of great help,' said James courteously.

'That's very kind of you,' Agatha said, getting to her feet and gathering up her handbag and gloves. 'But I don't see—'

'My powers of observation,' she cried. 'I would make a very good detective. Now, now, Mr Lacey,' she said roguishly, 'you have already marked me down as an expert sleuth!'

'Quite,' he said hastily. He took out a card and gave it to her. 'If you find anything, I will be at this address.'

After they had gone, Miss Purvey paced up and down her small cottage living-room. She felt excited, elated. That handsome Mr Lacey had looked at her in *such* a way! She walked to the window and peered up, rubbing the glass. The mist had taken on a yellowish light

98

showing that, far above, the sun was trying to struggle through.

Miss Purvey had a sudden longing for the lights and shops of Mircester. She had one close friend, Belinda Humphries, who ran a small dress shop in a shopping arcade in the town. Miss Purvey decided to go and see her, relishing the joys of describing James Lacey and the way he had looked at her. Of course, he had had Mrs Raisin with him, but she had asked him in the kitchen if they were going to be married after all and he had said quietly, 'Not now,' and she, Miss Purvey, was only a teensy bit older than Mrs Raisin.

She put on her coat and that sort of felt hat beloved by middle-class Englishwomen and damned as 'sensible', and made her way out to her Ford Escort, which was parked on the road outside the cottage.

Driving slowly and carefully, she joined the dual carriageway some miles outside the village, and moving into the fast lane, drove at a steady thirty miles per hour, seemingly deaf to the furious horns and flashing lights of the drivers behind her.

To her dismay, the fog began to thicken as she approached Mircester. She found a parking place in the central square, got out, locked her car and went to the shopping arcade. A neat sign hanging on the glass door said CLOSED. She gave a little cluck of dismay. She had forgotten it was half-day in Mircester.

She felt too strung up to go home. Of course she could have gone to Belinda's cottage, but that lay in a village twenty miles in the opposite direction out of Mircester from where she herself lived.

Miss Purvey decided to treat herself to a visit to the cinema. A Bruce Willis *Die Hard* movie was showing and Miss Purvey found Bruce Willis exciting. She had seen it before but knew she would enjoy seeing it again.

She bought a ticket at the kiosk and took a seat in the still-lit cinema. The programme was due to start in a few minutes.

Miss Purvey settled down and took a packet of strong peppermints out of her handbag, extracted one and popped it in her mouth. There were not many people in the cinema. She twisted round to see if there was any-one she knew and then her gaze fastened on the person in the row behind her, a little to her left. She turned away and then stiffened in her seat. Surely she had seen that face before.

She twisted round again and said in her loud, plummy voice, 'I've seen you somewhere before, haven't I?'

Rose, the usherette, was fifty-something, with bad feet. The days when usherettes were pert young things with trays of ices had long gone. The ices and popcorn were bought at a kiosk in the foyer, and inside, tired middle-aged women showed people to their seats and then searched while the cinema was empty to make sure no one had left anything valuable.

Rose saw the solitary figure sitting in the middle of

100

one of the rows in the centre and thought, here's another old-age pensioner fallen asleep. It was hard to be patient with these old people. Some of them didn't even know where they were or who they were when they woke up. The Cotswolds were turning into geriatric country.

She edged along the row behind the still figure and, leaning forward, shook one shoulder. It was like a Hitchcock movie, thought Rose, her heart leaping into her mouth. The figure slowly keeled sideways. Rose gasped, leaned over and shone her torch into the figure's face, for although the lights were on in the cinema, they were still quite dim.

The bulging eyes of Miss Purvey stared glassily back at her. A scarf was twisted savagely around the old scrawny neck.

Shock takes people in strange ways. Rose walked quickly to the foyer and told her fellow usherette to call the manager, and then she phoned the police. She told the man in the ticket office to come out and close the cinema doors and not let anyone else in. Then she lit a cigarette and waited. The police and an ambulance arrived, the CID arrived, the pathologist, and then the forensic team.

Rose told her story several times, was taken to the police station, where she repeated everything again, and then signed a statement.

She accepted a lift home in a police car and told the pretty young policewoman that she would be perfectly all right after she had had a cup of tea.

When she let herself into her house, her husband shambled out of the living-room. He was wearing his favourite old moth-eaten cardigan and he had bits of boiled egg stuck to his moustache.

'I hate you!' screamed Rose, and then she began to cry.

Chapter Five

James and Agatha walked through the fog back to Lilac Lane from the Red Lion that evening. They were silent. The villagers had decided that they were not murder suspects and so, instead of a chilly silence, they had received a warm greeting and then had had to endure a heavy sort of banter, being teased about when they were going to tell everyone the date of their wedding day.

James had not wanted to say firmly that he would never marry Agatha because that would have been rude, and so it was the blunt Agatha who had suddenly said loudly, 'We're not suited; we're not marrying, and that's that!'

And instead of being grateful to her for having sorted the whole business out, James felt obscurely that Agatha had given him a public rejection and was in a mood remarkably like a sulk.

Agatha grabbed his arm. 'Look!' she cried.

Under the security light outside James's door stood Detective Chief Inspector Wilkes, Bill Wong and Maddie.

'What's happened now?' asked James. 'Oh, God, I hope that Purvey woman hasn't committed suicide as well.'

Wilkes waited until they approached and then said, 'We'd better go inside.'

James let them in. They all stood around in the living-room.

'Sit down,' said Wilkes, his dark face serious. 'This might take some time. Did you call on a Miss Janet Purvey today?'

'Yes,' said Agatha. 'What is this about?'

'And where were you both this afternoon?'

'Before you go any further,' said James, 'I thought it was only in the movies that the police keep asking questions without telling anyone the real reason they are being questioned. So, out with it! Something awful has obviously happened to Miss Purvey.'

Bill Wong spoke up, his narrow eyes scanning both their faces. 'Miss Purvey was found strangled in the Imperial Cinema in Mircester this afternoon. So we must ask again, what were you both doing this afternoon?'

'You should know, Bill, that neither of us could have anything to do with her murder,' exclaimed Agatha.

'Just answer the question.' Maddie, her voice flat and hard.

'Yes, we saw Miss Purvey this morning,' said James. 'As far as we could gather, she had not been blackmailed, nor had she had much to do with either Mrs Gore-Appleton or Jimmy Raisin when she was at the health farm. After we left her, we stopped at a pub over in Ancombe for sandwiches, then we came back here. Agatha went into Moreton to do some shopping and I remained here. Mrs Bloxby called on me when Agatha was out and stayed for coffee.'

Bill turned to Agatha. 'Did anyone see you in Moreton?'

'Of course,' said Agatha. 'I went into Drury's, the butcher's, and then to Budgen's supermarket . . . oh, and then I went to that bookshop in the arcade. Then I had a coffee at the Market House Tea Room. People should remember me.'

'We'll check all that,' said Maddie and Agatha threw her a look of pure dislike.

Wilkes leaned forward. 'So to get back to the beginning. I gather Wong here told you not to do any more amateur detecting. But you had to go ahead, did you not? So begin at the beginning of your visit to Miss Purvey.'

James described all they had talked about but with one important omission that Agatha noticed although she kept quiet about it. He said nothing about Miss Purvey's wanting to play detective as well.

Wilkes then turned to Agatha and she had to tell her version of events.

The questioning went on and on. Finally Wilkes said, 'We'll need you both to come to the station and make a statement. Another death is just too much to swallow.

Like I said, I gather that Wong here told you to mind your own business and leave the detecting to the police.'

'Why did she go to Mircester after we left her?' asked Agatha.

Wilkes sighed. 'Presumably to go to the cinema. We can only guess the rest. She may have been holding something back and telephoned someone and arranged to meet them. Or someone saw her in the cinema, recognized her and judged her to be a threat. Just leave things to us.'

They all asked more questions before taking their leave.

Agatha and James stared at each other in gloomy silence.

At last James said, 'Look, Agatha, none of this is our fault. We didn't strangle her. But there is one good thing, if you can call it good, that will come out of all this. Press interest in the case will be renewed. They'll run that interview with us. People will know we are looking for Mrs Gore-Appleton, and someone is bound to come forward.'

'I wish the whole mess were over with,' said Agatha wearily. 'Perhaps we should leave the whole thing to the police.'

'Well, we've only got one more name,' pointed out James. 'There's a Mrs Gloria Comfort and she lives right in Mircester, near the abbey. And even if *The Bugle* doesn't run the story, some other newspaper will want to talk to you. It would take a world catastrophe to knock this out of the papers.'

The next morning James rose early and went out and bought all the newspapers. Black headlines screamed at him. Yeltsin had been overthrown. The generals in Moscow had made a coup. The Cold War was on again. The papers were full of reports on the front pages, and on the inside were endless articles by pundits. The murder of one elderly spinster in Mircester rated only a small paragraph in each. The rump of Serbia was supporting the generals. Russia was beginning to be torn apart by civil war.

He took the newspapers back to Agatha, who was playing with her cats on his kitchen floor. She rose to her feet and studied them in silence.

'At least,' said Agatha at last, 'we can go on detecting. If we had been the focus of press attention, it would have been hard to do.'

They talked about the world situation and then decided they might as well go into Mircester and make their statements, go somewhere for lunch, and then call on Mrs Gloria Comfort.

Maddie and Bill Wong were having a cup of tea in the canteen later that day. It was the first time since interviewing Agatha and James that they had been able to have a private conversation.

'So what do you think of your precious Agatha Raisin now?' demanded Maddie. 'That woman's like a vulture. Dead bodies wherever she goes.'

'That's a bit hard,' protested Bill. 'Their visit to Derrington may have touched off his suicide, but they were only a bit ahead of us and if the old boy was going to top himself, he would have done it sooner or later. And they had nothing to do with the murder of Miss Purvey. Agatha's alibi checks out. Look, Maddie, I must make one thing clear. Agatha's a friend of mine and I wish you'd stop bitching about her. I don't know if she exactly solved those last crimes, but she made things happen by poking her nose in; otherwise we'd never have got to the murderers.'

'I'm entitled to my own opinion,' said Maddie. 'Look at her odd relationship with Lacey. Their engagement breaks up because she's lied to him and yet they're living together.'

'I think they're very well suited,' mumbled Bill. He had invited Maggie home to meet his parents for dinner that very evening and he did not want anything to go wrong. 'Can't we just agree to disagree?'

'Have it your way. Haven't got the hots for old Agatha, have you?'

'She's old enough to be my mother!'

'Just wondered.'

Bill had been looking forward to showing off Maddie to his parents. Now a worm of uneasiness was beginning to wriggle in his brain. Could it be that his darling was, well, just a tiny bit abrasive?

Agatha and James drove in the direction of Mircester. The fog had lifted and it was a beautiful autumn day. The hedgerows were bright with hawthorn berries, and red-and-gold trees lined the edges of brown ploughed fields.

'The country doesn't seem beautiful at first,' said Agatha. 'I used to long for London. Then I got used to it. I started noticing the changing seasons, and then it began to look beautiful, like watching a series of landscape paintings, one after another. Except for those clouds. Someone ought to do something about those clouds, James. They're like those neat and regular watercolour ones painted by the Cotswold amateurs. The light is different, too. It sort of *slants* in the autumn.' Shafts of golden sunlight cut through the trees on to the winding road ahead. James braked sharply as a clumsy pheasant dithered about in front of his wheels which crunched on a carpet of beech nuts.

'I don't often want to put the clock back,' said Agatha in a small voice. 'But on days like this, I wish I had never got into this mess, and I know I won't be free until it's over. I can't even grieve for Jimmy. I think he'd turned into a right bad lot and if he hadn't been so bad, he would be alive and kicking. I could deal with a live Jimmy and get him out of my hair forever, but I can't fight a dead man. He came between us, James.'

'You put him there, Agatha. If you had found out his existence, we could have dealt with it.'

Agatha gave a small dry sob.

James took one hand off the steering wheel and gave her a quick hug. 'You need to give me time,' he said, and Agatha's heart suddenly rocketed with hope, like another pheasant which flew up at their approach and sailed over a hedge.

They received a setback after they had made their statements at police headquarters and gone in search of Mrs Gloria Comfort. They learned from neighbours that she had moved to one of the outlying villages. No one knew her new address but one of the neighbours remembered the house had been sold by Whitney and Dobster, estate agents.

At the estate agents', they found to their relief that the man who had organized the sale of Mrs Comfort's house in Mircester was still working there and cheerfully accepted their story that they were old friends trying to get in touch with her. He produced an address in Ancombe.

'Well!' exclaimed Agatha outside the estate agents' office. 'That's *very* close to Carsely, and to the scene of Jimmy's murder, too. Do you think the police will have been there before us?'

110

'Don't know. They always have such a lot of red tape to get through and we don't.'

Agatha suddenly hesitated. 'They'll be furious if they arrive and find us there.'

'It's getting late. They've either been there or they're getting there tomorrow.'

Ancombe was one of those Cotswold villages about the size of Broad Campden that seemed too perfect to be true. Very small but with an old church in the centre, thatched cottages, beautiful gardens, and everything with a manicured air.

Mrs Gloria Comfort lived in one of the prettiest of the thatched cottages under the shadow of the church. There was no answer to the door. 'Let's try round the back,' said James. 'I can hear some noises coming from there.'

'Probably writhing in her death agonies,' said Agatha gloomily.

They walked up the narrow path which led to the back garden. A plump blonde woman was weeding a flowerbed. 'Excuse me,' began James, and she rose and turned around.

Her hair was gloriously bleached blonde, not a dark root showing, but her middle-aged face was puffy and her eyes held that glittering look caused by a film of moisture, the sign of a heavy drinker. She was dressed unsuitably for gardening in a sort of Lady Tart outfit of

111

tightly tailored tweed jacket and skirt, frilly white blouse, pearls and high heels.

'Mrs Comfort?' said James.

'Are you collecting for something?'

'No, I am James Lacey and this is Agatha Raisin.'

'Oh, dear, you're the wife of that man who was murdered. You'd better come indoors.' She teetered across the lawn, her spiked heels making holes in the green turf. 'Good for the lawn,' she remarked. 'It aerates it.'

Indoors was in keeping with her dress. Everything was amazingly vulgar. Awful ruched curtains at the windows, fake horse brasses, fake old masters on the walls, and a padded white leather bar in one corner of the living-room. Mrs Comfort headed straight for the bar. 'Drink?'

Agatha said she would have a gin and tonic, and James, a whisky.

'Now,' Mrs Comfort said, perching on the very edge of an overstuffed sofa, 'what's this all about?'

'You were at the health farm at the same time as Jimmy,' began Agatha. 'We're interested in who he talked to. We're also very interested in the woman who accompanied him, a Mrs Gore-Appleton.'

Mrs Comfort took a strong pull of the very dark liquid in her glass. Then she said, 'It's hard to remember. It all seems so long ago. Jimmy Raisin was hailed as one of the successes. He arrived looking like a wreck, and by the end of the first week he looked like a different man. I can't tell you anything about Mrs Gore-Appleton.

112

I didn't talk to her much except for the odd remark about the weather and how awful it was to feel so hungry – that sort of thing. I can't really be of much help to you, I'm afraid.'

James said, 'Have the police been to see you yet?'

'No. Why should they want to see me? Oh, because of Mr Raisin being murdered.'

'It's not as simple as that. You may not have noticed in the newspapers today because of all the world news, but a certain Miss Purvey was murdered in Mircester.'

'Purvey? Purvey! She was there at the health farm. Thin spinster. But surely that has nothing to do with anything.'

'Jimmy Raisin was a blackmailer,' said Agatha.

Mrs Comfort choked on her drink and then appeared to rally. 'Really?' she said brightly. 'How sickening.'

Agatha took a gamble. 'The real reason we are here is because we think he may have been blackmailing you.'

'How dare you! There is nothing about me that anyone could blackmail me about. I think you should both go.'

Mrs Comfort got to her feet. They rose as well. 'You would not like to try the real story out on us first?' asked James gently.

'What do you mean, on you first?'

'The police will be here soon and they will ask you the same questions. Then they will check your bank statements to see if you have been drawing out regular

113

sums of money to pay blackmail, or if you ever issued a cheque to Jimmy Raisin.'

She sat down as if her legs had suddenly given way. Her puffy face crumpled and she looked about to cry. Agatha and James slowly sat down again.

She mutely held out her now empty glass to James. He took it, sniffed it, and then went behind the white leather bar and filled it with neat whisky and carried it back to her. They waited while she drank in silence and then she said, 'Why not hear it all?

'As I said, Jimmy Raisin was a wreck when he first came, but he soon smartened up. He was charming and amusing and . . . well, the others seemed a lot of stuffed shirts, and because I was a woman on my own, I was put at the same table as Miss Purvey, and that made me feel like shit.

'Jimmy started to flirt with me and then he said he'd been down to the village that afternoon and he had a couple of Cornish pasties in his room. I went along to have one because I was so hungry and we were giggling like schoolchildren at a midnight feast. One thing led to another and we ended up spending the night together. We were very civilized about it the next day. As far as I was concerned, it was a one-night stand. I was married, and happily married, too, but those Cornish pasties had seduced me in the same way as vintage champagne would have done on another occasion.'

She paused to drink more whisky thirstily.

'Do you know, I almost forgot about the whole

episode? It meant that little. Then one day, when my husband had just gone off to work – we were living in Mircester then – Jimmy turned up. He said that unless I paid him, he would tell my husband about our night together. I told him to get lost. It was his word against mine, and I would deny the whole thing. But he wrote to my husband and described certain details about me and . . . and . . . my husband divorced me.'

There was a long silence.

Agatha said quietly, 'Why did you tell us this? You paid him nothing, so there would be no way anyone could find out anything from your bank statements.'

She shrugged wearily. 'I've never told anyone. Can you imagine the shame? Thirty years of married life down the tubes, just like that. I *hated* Jimmy Raisin, but I didn't kill him. I'm too much of a wimp. I was shattered. All those years of marriage, and Geoffrey, my husband, wouldn't forgive me. He rushed the divorce through. I was amazed at the generous settlement, and then I found out why. I found out why after the divorce because that's when your best friends come forward and tell you what they should have told you before. He'd been having an affair with a woman in his office and all I did was hand him a big golden opportunity on a plate.'

'This Mrs Gore-Appleton,' said James. 'Didn't Jimmy talk about her, explain to you why he was there with her?'

'He said she was some sort of do-gooder who was paying for his treatment, but that was all. We didn't talk

115

much except about the health farm and joked about the awful exercises and the food.'

She began to cry quietly. 'We're sorry,' said Agatha. 'We're just trying to find out who murdered Jimmy.'

She dried her eyes and blew her nose. 'Why? Who cares?'

'Until we find out who murdered him, we're all suspects, even you.'

Her eyes widened in alarm. 'I shouldn't have told you about sleeping with Jimmy. You won't tell the police?'

And the two amateur detectives, who were still smarting over having been told to keep out of the investigations, both nodded their heads. 'We won't tell,' said Agatha. She fished in her handbag and found one of her cards. 'Here's my address and number. If you can think of any little thing that might help, please let me know.'

'All right. I'm thinking already.'

'You see,' said James, 'if we could find this Mrs Gore-Appleton, I feel we could get somewhere. There's no evidence that she was in on this blackmailing lark. Jimmy was taking only five hundred pounds a month from Sir Desmond Derrington. Mrs Gore-Appleton gave an address in Mayfair to the health farm. Mind you, it seems to have been a false address, but believe me, if she had been in on the act, I feel the demand would have been higher. I don't know why. Just an idea. What was she like?'

Mrs Comfort frowned. 'Let me see ... blonde, good figure, bit muscular, loud laugh, sort of plummy voice, was very close to Jimmy but more like a mother looking after her child.'

James remembered Miss Purvey saying that she had seen Jimmy going into Mrs Gore-Appleton's bedroom one night but kept silent. 'She didn't speak to me much or to anyone else, for that matter,' Mrs Comfort went on. 'Apart from Jimmy, that is.' Her watery eyes suddenly focused sharply on Agatha. 'Why did you marry him?'

Agatha remembered Jimmy when they had first married – reckless, handsome, full of fun. Then Jimmy slowly sinking into alcoholic stupors while she worked hard as a waitress, Jimmy surfacing occasionally from an alcoholic coma to beat her. Their marriage had been short and violent and she could still remember that feeling of glorious freedom when she had walked out on him for the last time, never to return.

'I was very young,' she said. 'Jimmy began to drink heavily soon after we were married and so I left him. End of story.'

James said suddenly, 'Be careful, Mrs Comfort.'

'Why?'

'There's a murderer at large and it's someone who was at that health farm, I'm sure of it. Someone recognized Miss Purvey and decided to shut her up. It could be that Jimmy had something on Miss Purvey and was blackmailing her. That someone could be carrying on the blackmail where Jimmy left off. Are you sure there is

117

nothing else you can remember, however small and insignificant it might seem, which might help?'

'There was only one stupid thing,' she said. 'It's about Mrs Gore-Appleton.'

'What's that?' asked Agatha eagerly.

'Well, there were times when I thought she would have made a very good man.'

James and Agatha stared at her in surprise.

'It's just a feeling. She had a very muscular body. She wasn't exactly mannish. It was just something about her. Have you checked out everyone else who was there at the same time as me?'

James shook his head. 'Just the ones who lived near Mircester. There was Sir Desmond. Then there was Miss Purvey, and then yourself.'

'But why did you assume the murderer was someone from near Mircester?

'Because Jimmy Raisin was murdered in Carsely. It must have been someone who lives locally.'

'But if you're dealing with a blackmailer, or maybe a couple of blackmailers,' protested Mrs Comfort, 'then they could have followed their victims to London or Manchester or wherever! Then Jimmy Raisin could have let slip that he was going to your wedding.'

'I don't like that idea,' said Agatha. 'A friend of ours got a detective to find Jimmy Raisin and he was living in a packing-case at Waterloo. He was hardly in a state to go around blackmailing anyone.'

'But when he heard you were getting married, he managed to get down to Mircester all right. He could have sobered up enough to go out from his packing-case to try one of his old victims and then said something like, oh, "I'm going to Mircester."'

Agatha groaned. 'How many people were there at the same time as you?'

'Not many. It's so expensive. Only about thirty of us.'

'Thirty,' echoed Agatha in a hollow voice.

'It's got to be someone local,' insisted James.

'But who?' demanded Agatha. 'It's obviously not Mrs Comfort here. Miss Purvey is dead. Sir Desmond is dead. Who's left?'

'Both of you,' suggested Mrs Comfort with a tinge of malice in her voice.

'Or Lady Derrington,' said James. 'What about Lady Derrington? She may have known about the blackmail all along and decided to get rid of Jimmy herself.'

'Or what about Sir Desmond?' put in Agatha. 'He could have killed Jimmy and then committed suicide in a fit of remorse.'

'So who killed Miss Purvey?'

'That could have been Lady Derrington,' said Agatha eagerly. 'Miss Purvey said she was going to do some detecting. What if she knew something about the Derringtons?'

'Or,' said Mrs Comfort, 'it could have been that woman Derrington was having an affair with.'

They both looked at her in surprise. Then James said slowly, 'We never thought of her.'

Mrs Comfort suddenly stood up. 'Well, if that's all . . .?'

They got to their feet as well, thanked her for her hospitality, put their glasses on the horrible bar, and left.

Mrs Comfort watched them go, watched them get into James's car, watched them drive off. Then she picked up the phone.

Maddie was seated that evening at the Wongs' family dining table and wondering how soon she could escape. That Bill was immensely fond of his parents was transparently easy to see. But Maddie wondered why. Mrs Wong was a massive, discontented Gloucestershire woman and his father a morose Hong Kong Chinese. The food was frightful: microwaved steak and kidney pie with potatoes made from that dehydrated stuff that comes in a packet – just add water – and tinned green peas of the type that ooze a lake of green dye all over the plate. The wine was a sweet Sauternes.

Maddie was beginning to think that Bill Wong was not worth all this effort. He was reckoned to be one of the brightest detectives on the force. Maddie was ambitious. She had thought that if she courted Bill, had an affair with Bill, kept close to Bill, then she could pick his brain, maybe solve the case, and get the kudos. But the murder case was still plodding its way through reams of slow, painstaking investigation, and there didn't seem to be a break anywhere, nor did Bill appear to have been struck by any bright ideas.

She suddenly realized that Mrs Wong was addressing her. 'Our Bill likes his food,' said Mrs Wong, 'so you see he gets it.'

'The police canteen looks after his needs,' said Maddie.

'Mother means when you two are married,' said Mr Wong.

Maddie was tough, Maddie was selfish and Maddie was strong, but at those words she felt a stab of panic. Of course she should have realized what an invitation to dinner in the Wong family home would mean.

'We are not getting married,' she said firmly.

'I haven't even asked her yet,' said Bill with an uneasy laugh.

'Not that we think you're old enough to get married,' Mrs Wong ploughed on. 'You young people are always rushing into things. Course, as me and Dad were saying the other day, grandchildren would be nice. I always wanted a little girl,' she said to Maddie, who was now staring at her plate in fixed embarrassment.

Maddie was then interrogated about her parents, her brother and sister, where they all lived, and whether she intended to remain in her job after she was married to Bill.

'Look,' said Maddie, her own voice sounding shrill in her ears, 'there's been a misunderstanding. I am not going to marry Bill or anyone else at the moment. Now can we change the subject?'

Mr Wong looked insulted and Bill, miserable. He could not in his heart blame his parents, for had he not told them that Maddie was the only girl for him? But Bill could never find it in his heart to blame his parents for anything.

Maddie was only grateful that she had driven herself to Bill's home. She pleaded a headache directly after dinner and then Bill walked her out to her car.

'You shouldn't have given them the impression we were to be married,' said Maddie harshly.

Bill looked embarrassed. 'Well, they are apt to look at every girl I bring home as a possible daughter-in-law. Don't let it spoil things, Maddie.'

'Goodnight.'

'When will I see you again?'

'At police headquarters tomorrow.'

'You know what I mean.'

'I'm going to be awfully busy in my spare time.' Maddie slid neatly into the driving seat, closed the door on Bill's protest and drove off, without, his policeman's mind noticed, putting her seat-belt on.

He stood there feeling lost. He thought of Agatha and wished she were back in her own cottage, without James. He suddenly wanted to talk to Agatha. She wasn't married to James. Perhaps he could get her to come to the pub with him.

* * *

122

James looked surprised when Bill Wong, with the air of a schoolboy asking if a mate could come out and play, requested to see Agatha for a private conversation.

Agatha appeared in the doorway as well. 'Come in,' said James. 'I'll go out for a walk if you like.'

'No, I'll take Agatha to the pub, if that's all right.'

'Catch up with you later,' said James.

'Leave your car,' said Agatha, joining Bill. 'We'll walk to the Red Lion.'

'I would rather go somewhere more private,' said Bill. 'I don't want Lacey to join us.'

When she was in his car, Agatha asked nervously, 'Am I in trouble?'

He gave her a sad little smile. 'No, I think I am. We'll go to the Royal White Hart in Moreton. Wait till we get there.'

The bar for once was comparatively empty. Autumn had come, the leaves were falling and the tourists had disappeared. One of the difficulties of living in a beauty spot like the Cotswolds, reflected Agatha, was that for a good part of the year it was swamped with tourists; but then one couldn't complain: anyone moving out of his own village automatically became a tourist.

They took seats at the corner of one of the large tables by the fireplace, where a stack of logs was burning brightly.

'So,' said Agatha, 'what's up? No one else murdered, I hope?'

He shook his head. 'It's me and Maddie.'

123

Agatha felt an irrational stab of jealousy and then reminded herself severely that Bill was in his twenties and she in her fifties. 'What's Hatchet Face been up to then?' she asked.

Bill grinned. 'I'd almost forgotten how much I liked you.'

Agatha suddenly felt tears welling up in her eyes and fought them back. She wondered if she would ever get used to this new feeling of being liked. It seemed that during her long business life, no one had ever liked Agatha Raisin, and with good reason. The old Agatha had not been either likeable or lovable.

'Go on,' she said.

Bill looked at the firelight shining in the contents of his half-pint glass and said, 'You know I was keen on Maddie.'

'Yes.'

Bill sighed. 'You know something, Agatha, I was born too late. There's something awfully old-fashioned about me. I think when a woman goes to bed with me that it means some sort of commitment.'

'And it didn't?'

'I thought it did. I had the wedding all planned, I had even begun to look at houses. I'd totally forgotten that I had not mentioned any of those rosy dreams to Maddie. I invited her home this evening to meet my parents.'

Agatha was about to say, oh dear, but bit it back. She privately thought that Mr and Mrs Wong would be enough to kill love in even the most romantic female breast.

'Well, you know what Mum and Dad are like. They just come out with things. It's not their fault they're so honest.'

It's their fault they're so bloody rude, thought Agatha, but said nothing.

'So Mum assumed we were going to get married, and to tell the truth, I had pretty much assumed the same thing. But Maddie got scared off and I don't think she's going to see me again, outside police work. The pain's awful, Agatha. She was so fed up with me, she drove off without even her seat-belt on.'

'Maybe she'll be all right tomorrow,' said Agatha and then cursed herself for raising false hopes.

His face brightened for a moment and then fell. 'No, I have a gut feeling it's over. You know what rejection feels like, Agatha.'

Agatha pressed his hand, and those tears that she could now not hold back welled up and spilled over on to her cheeks.

'Oh, Agatha,' said Bill, 'I didn't mean to make you cry.'

But Agatha was crying for herself, for losing James, for what seemed to her years of a wasted loveless life devoted to work.

She dried her eyes and pulled herself together with an effort. 'All I can suggest, Bill, is that when you see her tomorrow, you're just as friendly and casual and normal as possible, so that she has nothing to react against.

Maybe take some other girl out. But if she still wants you, she'll let you know. If not, then you'll save face.'

Bill grinned. 'I'm only half Chinese and my poor soul is pure Gloucestershire. You're right. But how can any woman make love, spend nights, and then simply walk off, just like that?'

Because she thought you were expendable, thought Agatha. Because she thought you would further her career if she could pick your brains, but after meeting your parents and being threatened with marriage, she thought it was all just not worth the effort. Because she's a cold bitch. There are gold-diggers and career-diggers, and your precious Maddie is a career-digger. Aloud she said, 'A lot of women are surprisingly terrified of marriage, particularly if they are interested in their jobs. But I don't suppose that makes you feel any better. Rejection is a pain in the bum. Have another drink, something stronger.'

'I'm driving.'

'And I feel like getting drunk,' said Agatha. 'We'll take a cab back. James can drive you back to Mircester and then take a cab home.'

'Hadn't you better phone him and ask him?'

'No, he'll do it. Let's drink. Change over to the hard stuff.'

James Lacey was none too pleased to find a tipsy Agatha and Bill weaving on his doorstep at half past eleven at night and to learn that he had to drive Bill to Mircester and then pay for a cab back. Nor was he pleased that Agatha and Bill travelled in the back seat with their arms around each other, roaring out raucous songs.

His face stiff with disapproval, he drove Bill home in Bill's car, which he had picked up outside the White Hart. Bill phoned for a cab. James planned to give Agatha a piece of his mind on the road home, but she promptly fell asleep and snored, with her head lolling against his shoulder.

After having paid the cab, driven his own car from Moreton, and helped Agatha indoors and upstairs to her bedroom, he went down to the living-room, feeling angry and left out. Why should Wong want to discuss the case with Agatha and leave him out in the cold? What was going on there?

Chapter Six

In the morning, a hung-over Agatha Raisin crept down-stairs to receive a taste of what marriage to James might have been like.

'That was incredibly selfish behaviour last night, Agatha. You should be ashamed of yourself!'

'James, can't you wait till I get a cup of coffee?'

'Selfish!' James paced up and down the small kitchen. 'I thought we were in this investigation together, and yet you two go off. I went to the Red Lion but you hadn't gone there. The next thing I know, you are both back here drunk at closing time. I have to run you back to Moreton, leave my car, run Bill home, get a cab back to Moreton to pick up my own car – well, it's just too much.'

Agatha poured a cup of coffee with a shaking hand and then lit a cigarette. James angrily jerked open the kitchen window, letting in a blast of cold autumn air. 'And that's a filthy habit, Agatha. This whole house is beginning to stink of cigarette smoke.'

'Leave me alone,' wailed Agatha, slumping down at the kitchen table.

There was a ring at the bell. James stumped off to answer it. Soon he was back. 'It's that Mrs Hardy for you. I didn't invite her in.'

Curiosity momentarily banishing her pounding hangover, Agatha went to the door.

'Good morning,' said Mrs Hardy. 'I am reconsidering your offer.'

Hope shone in Agatha's eyes. 'You mean I can buy my cottage back?'

'If you wish.'

'I'll get dressed and come along and see you,' said Agatha eagerly.

'Don't take all day about it. I'm going out.'

Agatha went upstairs and hurriedly washed and dressed. 'Going next door,' she called to James. 'The Hardy woman's prepared to sell.'

Seated a few minutes later in Mrs Hardy's kitchen and studying her covertly, Agatha wondered if she herself in the not-so-far-off days had been a bit like this Mrs Hardy, blunt and abrasive.

'Why do you want to sell?' asked Agatha.

'Does it matter? Carsely does not suit.' She poured herself a cup of coffee but did not offer Agatha any.

So they got down to business. Agatha at last rose at the end of it, feeling weak and not only with a hangover. Mrs Hardy drove a hard bargain. Agatha would have to pay a lot more to get her cottage back than Mrs Hardy had given her for it. Later, Agatha was to wonder why she had not tried to hold off a little, to drive the price down, but she was so eager to have her old home back and get out from living with James that she had agreed to the price Mrs Hardy had named.

'Great news,' she said to James when she returned. 'The Hardy creature is selling me back my cottage.'

'How much?'

'A lot.'

'Is it worth it, Agatha? You can stay here as long as you like.'

Agatha threw him a frustrated look. She could not be herself, living with James. He did most of the cooking and cleaning. She realized that even if they had married, it would probably have been just the same. She lived as if in a hotel, carefully keeping her clothes and belongings to the spare room; trying to remember to scrub out the bath every time, realizing that she was quite a messy person. Housekeepers, thought Agatha, were born, not made. Being a good housekeeper was a separate talent, like being a ballet dancer or opera singer. Being brought up in a slum, where food came out of cans and cleaning was sporadic and clothes often were not washed from one week to the other, didn't help one in future life. While she had had her own house, James had only seen the best of her. Had she suffered then from this hangover, she would have stayed indoors until she got rid of it, and then emerged, made up and dressed to kill. She ran an exploratory finger over her upper lip. A stiff little

130

couple of hairs were sprouting there. She felt they were waving their antennae at James like insects. She made a hurried excuse and went up to the bathroom, waxed her upper lip clean, opened the bathroom window and tossed the wax out into the bushes, planning to retrieve it later and hide it in the kitchen garbage where James would not spot it. It's such hard work being middle-aged, thought Agatha bleakly, and it will get much worse when I'm old, what with farting and incontinence and falling hair and teeth. God, I wish I were dead. And on that cheerful thought she went back downstairs.

'Bill and I weren't talking about the case,' she said to James's rigid back as he stood over the cooker scrambling eggs. 'Maddie's rejected him and he is deeply hurt.'

'Oh.' James's back relaxed. 'And you didn't tell him about our visit to Gloria Comfort?'

'No,' said Agatha. 'We got drunk to comfort him. Stupid, I know, and you were really good to take him home. Maddie may be a pill, but he's mourning her all the same.'

James slid a plate of fluffy scrambled eggs under Agatha's nose. 'Eat that and you'll feel better.'

'Nothing will make me feel better but the passing of time and the first stiff Scotch,' said Agatha, but she managed to eat some of the egg and a piece of toast.

The doorbell went again and she clutched her head and groaned. 'If that's anyone for me, get rid of them, James. I can't even bear to see Mrs Bloxby.'

131

But James returned with Bill, Maddie and Wilkes. Agatha felt her stomach lurch.

'Now,' said Wilkes severely, 'I gather from descriptions received that you and Mr Lacey here called on a Mrs Gloria Comfort yesterday.'

Agatha bleakly marvelled at the life of the English village. It had seemed completely deserted when they had called on Mrs Comfort, but hidden eyes had probably taken in every detail of their appearance.

'She's not *dead*, is she?' asked Agatha.

'Mrs Gloria Comfort packed up after you left, deposited her keys at the local police station, and said she was going on holiday to Spain. She took a flight to Madrid from Heathrow, hired a car at the Madrid airport and took off for God knows where. Now what we want to know is what did you say to her?'

'And why,' said Maddie in a flat voice, 'were you calling on any suspect when you had been told not to?'

'It's a free country,' said Agatha. 'Anyway, she hadn't much to say. She said she wasn't being blackmailed by Jimmy, even after we told her the police would probably examine her bank accounts to make sure. She said nothing about going to Spain.'

The questioning began in earnest. They told them everything, except the bit about Mrs Comfort spending the night with Jimmy.

At last they rose to go. Maddie leaned over Agatha and said, 'Just butt out, will you?'

'Oh, go away,' snarled Agatha. 'Your face gives me a pain.'

Bill looked at Agatha bleakly, but said nothing.

After James had closed the door on them, Agatha said, 'That's a turn-up for the book. Why would she run like that? What had she to fear?'

'Let's go and break into her cottage tonight,' said James.

'What if we're caught? And look how many people seemed to notice our visit and describe us. What if they phone the police?'

'They won't see us if we go in the middle of the night.'

'Security lights? Burglar alarms?'

'She had neither. I noticed that.'

Agatha looked at him doubtfully. 'These Cotswold villages are crammed with geriatrics, James, and old people don't sleep much. They'd hear the car.'

'We'll drive a little way to Ancombe and then walk the rest. We'll wear dark clothes but nothing too sinister-looking in case someone meets us on the road. Now, if I were you, I would go back to bed and sleep off that hangover. You'll need all your wits about you tonight.'

Agatha felt better physically by that evening, but apprehensive about the night to come. She knew in her bones that if they were caught breaking into Mrs Comfort's cottage, they could certainly be arrested for that and also for interfering in police business. Roy Silver phoned

133

from London and Agatha asked him if he could check up on the woman who had posed as Lady Derrington at the health clinic and find out what he could.

They set out at two in the morning. James parked the car beside a farm gate outside the village and they got out and began to walk. It was a dark, moonless night with a rising wind. Beech nuts crunched under their feet and more beech nuts hurtled down from the trees which arched over the narrow road. 'I've never seen so many beech nuts,' complained Agatha. 'Is this the sign of a hard winter, or what?'

'Everything's always the sign of a hard winter in the country,' said James. 'If people go on saying it often enough, they're bound to be right one of those years. Shh, we're nearly at the village.'

They moved quietly. The darker bulk of the church rose against the black sky. 'Not a sign of life anywhere,' whispered James, but nervous Agatha was sure sleepless old people were sitting behind their net curtains, watching their approach with beady eyes. The silence seemed absolute. Nothing stirred except the wind in the trees.

James quietly opened the front gate to Mrs Comfort's cottage and once more they made their way around the back. Agatha was comforted somewhat by the secluded darkness of the garden.

James took out a pencil-torch and gave it to Agatha. 'Shine that at the door,' he whispered, taking out a bunch of lock-picks.

For the umpteenth time, Agatha wondered what a seemingly respectable retired colonel was doing with a bunch of lock-picks.

In the movies, locks were picked with amazing speed and ease. Agatha hugged herself and shivered as half an hour dragged past.

'How much longer are you going to be?' she hissed.

'Keep your hair on. I've done the Yale. It's the second lock that's the problem.'

A light came on in a cottage on the other side of the back garden, a shaft of yellow cutting through the sheltering trees. James froze and Agatha let out a little whimper of alarm. Then the light went out again and they were plunged back into comforting darkness.

At last, just when Agatha was about to suggest they give up the whole mad scheme, James gave a grunt of satisfaction and the door swung open.

He reached for Agatha's hand and led her in behind him, flashing the pen-light on and off.

'Upstairs,' said James. 'I didn't notice anywhere in the living-room where she might keep letters or papers.'

Soon the thin beam from his torch was flickering over the chaos of the bedroom. Drawers hung open at crazy angles and the wardrobe stood open as well.

'Someone has been here before us,' said Agatha. 'The police?'

'I think it's panic-packing. You sit on that chair over there by the window and peer through the curtains and keep a lookout and I'll search around.'

After searching through letters and papers in the dressing-table drawers, James gave a muffled exclamation and brought a letter over to Agatha. 'Get down on the floor while I shine the torch on this,' he said. 'It's worth reading.'

Agatha squatted down on the floor and read the letter.

Dear Gloria,

Please, please reconsider. I've said I'm sorry so many times. We had a good marriage and could have a good marriage again if only you would see me, listen to me. We could go away somewhere, anywhere you like, and mend fences. Just see me the once anyway. What harm could it do? You can't still be bitter after all this time. I love you.

Please call.
Geoffrey.

The letter had been typed on business paper, a Mircester firm called Potato Plus.

Agatha looked up in amazement. 'So what was all that about the ruined marriage when she could have had it all back? She must have gone off with him.'

'Looks like it. But let me have another look.'

After an hour he said, 'No, nothing else. I think we'd better leave it at that. Give me that letter, Agatha, and I'll put it back exactly as I found it.'

As they went down the stairs, Agatha suddenly grabbed his arm, making him jump.

'The living-room. She's got an answering machine. Let's check it for messages before we go.'

'All right,' said James. 'But I doubt if we'll learn more than we have. That letter from the husband was dated three days ago. It's clear to me she's gone off with him.'

They went into the living-room. James played back the answering machine. 'This is Jane,' said a voice. 'I'm sorry I was out when you called, Gloria. Yes, I'll look after your garden. I've still got your keys. Have a good trip. Bye.'

Then a man's voice. 'Hello, Basil here, sweetheart. I've got the tickets and I'll see you at Heathrow at four thirty at the check-in. Don't be late.'

They looked at each other in surprise. 'Basil?' exclaimed Agatha. 'But her husband's name is Geoffrey. And she must have phoned him after we left to arrange the trip because he says nothing about Madrid, only that he's got the tickets.'

'Let's just get out of here before our luck runs out,' said James. 'I'm tired of whispering.'

'Will it take ages for you to lock up?'

'No, that's the easy bit.'

Soon they were walking out of Ancombe, towards their car. 'I've been thinking,' said James as they drove off, 'that we've been concentrating on people who were blackmailed or used by Jimmy Raisin. We never really thought of the partners or spouses, except perhaps Lady Derrington. Look at it this way. Mrs Comfort is upset by our visit, though I don't know why. Her husband wants her back. But she phones Basil, someone she's obviously close enough to so that he promptly arranges they head off for Spain, just like that.'

'The police said she hired a car in Madrid. They didn't say anything about anyone being with her. Of course, this Basil could be married. They could have travelled separately on the plane, she hires the car and picks him up outside the airport. Easy. Oh, God, James, stop the car!'

He screeched to a halt. 'What's up?'

'That call from Basil was the last one. There were only two calls on that answering machine. If that was the very last call she got, we could dial 1471 and find out this Basil's phone number.'

'Agatha! That would mean picking those locks again. I daren't risk it. Look, this Jane female should be easy to find. We'll go back to Ancombe tomorrow. She'll probably know who it was.'

'But she might not be a close friend. She might just be some woman who looks after people's houses and gardens when they're away. Please, James.'

He set off again. 'No, Agatha, absolutely not. Trust me. This Jane will know.'

They found Jane easily enough after inquiring at the church the next morning. The verger told them that Jane Barclay was the lady they were looking for and directed them to her cottage.

Jane Barclay was a powerful, masculine-looking middle-aged woman with cropped grey hair.

It took them only a short time, during which Agatha slid the silk scarf from her neck and put it in her pocket, to establish that Jane Barclay was not an intimate friend of Mrs Gloria Comfort.

'The real reason we have come,' gushed Agatha, while James looked at her in surprise, 'is because I left my scarf at Gloria's yesterday. She told me you looked after the garden and the way she talked about you made us believe you were a close friend and might know exactly where in Spain she had gone. But you do have the keys. Could you be an angel and let us in so that I can look for it?'

'I suppose so,' said Jane. 'Who did you say you were?'

'Mr and Mrs Perth,' said James quickly, before Agatha could say anything. He was frightened that if she heard Agatha's name, she might be more cautious about letting the wife of a murdered man into that cottage.

'Have you any identification?'

Agatha's heart sank, but to her amazement James fished a card-case out of his inside pocket and extracted a card.

'Colonel and Mrs Perth,' Jane read aloud. 'From Stratford. She never mentioned you, but then I don't know her all that well. Come along. Don't take too long about it.'

They walked with her the short distance to Mrs Comfort's cottage. James kept glancing down at Agatha,

139

guessing that she wanted to get to that phone. When they entered the living-room, Agatha looked around brightly. 'Now where did I put my scarf. I know I left it here.'

James crossed to the window and looked out. 'The dahlias haven't been damaged by frost yet,' he said. 'They make a fine show.'

Jane Barclay crossed to join him. 'I planted those,' she said proudly. 'Mrs Comfort – Gloria – really doesn't know a thing about gardening.'

Agatha took the scarf from her pocket and thrust it down between the cushions of the sofa.

'I've found it,' she cried, fishing it out as Jane turned round. 'It must have slipped between the cushions.'

James was still at the window. 'Some of those roses could do with being cut back.'

'What? Where?' demanded Jane angrily. 'Those are the best-tended roses in the Cotswolds. I'll show you.'

'You go ahead,' said Agatha. 'I'll just powder my nose.'

Jane wasn't even listening to her. She was too angry at this slur on her gardening capabilities.

When they both walked out, Agatha quickly crossed to the phone and dialled 1471. She made a rapid note of the last caller's number and then went out to the garden, where James was saying plaintively, 'Well, bless me, what a splendid job you've done. Forgive me, Miss Barclay. It's my damned eyesight. Not as good as it was.'

Jane was mollified enough to talk for what seemed to Agatha an unconscionable time about gardening.

140

At last they thanked Jane and went back to their car. As soon as they were out of earshot, Agatha said excitedly, 'I got the number.'

'It may not be this mysterious Basil's number.' James drove a little way along the road and then stopped. 'Let me see it.'

Agatha gave him the slip of paper with the number on it. 'It's a Mircester number,' said James, 'but it could also belong to any of the villages just outside Mircester. How are we going to find out the address that goes with it?'

Agatha sat scowling horribly. 'I've got an idea,' she said at last. 'Any time I've been to police headquarters in Mircester to talk to Bill Wong or someone about a case, I've been put in an interview room and had to wait ages. The interview room has a phone. I could phone the operator and say I was a police detective, and before they get suspicious say something like, "Phone me back immediately at police headquarters on this extension."'

'Agatha, I forbid you to do anything so insane!'

'You *what*? Who the hell do you think you are to order me around?'

'See sense, woman. The one time someone will come to see you immediately is just when you don't want it. The phone will ring and someone like the dreadful Maddie will pick it up and promptly charge you with trying to impersonate a police officer.'

'One has,' said Agatha Raisin haughtily, 'to take risks in this business.'

141

'Oh, don't get carried away. All we've done so far is create mayhem. I'll drop you off home. I'm going to the market in Moreton to get fish for dinner. If time lies heavy on your hands, you might try a little weeding, *dear*. It has not escaped my notice that you treat my place like a hotel.'

'That's because it is your place,' said Agatha, deeply hurt. 'I can't wait to get my own home back.'

'Can't wait either,' said James, and they completed the drive home in bitter silence.

James went off to Moreton-in-Marsh and Agatha let herself in, smarting with hurt and fury. So this is what marriage would have been like? Being ordered about? How dare he. Well, she'd show him.

She went back out and got into her own car and drove as fast as she could to Mircester.

Feeling a bit nervous now, she approached the desk sergeant at Mircester police headquarters and said sweetly, 'I would like to see someone in connection with the murder of Jimmy Raisin.'

'It's Mrs Raisin, isn't it?'

'Yes.'

He lifted the flap, came round the desk and ushered her into an interview room off the entrance hall.

'Shouldn't be long,' he said cheerfully. 'Like a cup of tea?'

'No, thank you.'

He left and shut the door. Agatha seized the phone and dialled the operator. Nothing happened. Then she realized she probably had to dial 9 for an outside line and, hoping it was 9, tried again. The operator came on the line.

'This is Detective Sergeant Crumb,' said Agatha, quickly taking her alias from the remains of a biscuit on a plate on the desk. She gave the operator the number she had culled from Mrs Comfort's phone, asked for the name and address that went with it, and then gave her the number of the extension on the desk.

'We'll call you back,' said the operator.

And Agatha waited and waited.

Then panic took over. She lifted the phone off the desk and put it on the floor. She seized the desk and pushed it across the floor and rammed it against the door. She had just finished doing that when two things happened at once. Someone tried to get in and the phone rang.

Agatha dropped to her knees on the floor, grabbed the receiver and muttered hoarsely into it. 'Yes?'

'Detective Sergeant Crumb?'

'Yes, yes,' hissed Agatha as she heard Maddie's voice calling from the other side of the door, 'Mrs Raisin? Are you in there? This door's jammed.'

'The name and address you require is Basil Morton, number six, The Loanings, London Road, Mircester.'

'Thanks,' said Agatha.

She moved the desk and lay down alongside the door, just as she heard Maddie shouting, 'Dave, come and help me with this door.'

143

Agatha groaned theatrically. 'Are you all right?' Maddie called, her voice sharp more with suspicion than with concern.

'I fainted,' called Agatha. 'I'll move. I'm blocking the door.'

She got to her feet and stood back as Maddie, with a policeman behind her, opened the door. Maddie's eyes went straight to Agatha's flushed face and then to the phone, which was lying on the floor.

'You don't look at all like a woman who has just recovered from a faint,' snapped Maddie. 'And what's that phone doing on the floor? And didn't I hear it ringing?'

'I must have dragged it off the desk when I fell. It only rang a couple of times and then stopped.'

'And it landed right side up with the receiver still in place?'

'Odd, that,' said Agatha. She put her hand to her head. 'I feel very hot. Could I have a glass of water?'

'Get it,' Maddie ordered the policeman. 'It's probably a menopausal hot flush.'

Agatha glared at her, hating her.

'So let's cut the crap, Mrs Raisin. Why are you here?'

'If that's your attitude, I think I'd rather speak to Bill.'

'Bill's out on a job, and either you speak to me or I'll have you for wasting police time.'

'It's a wonder you ever solve anything,' said Agatha, 'considering the way you put people's backs up.'

The policeman came in with the glass of water and

handed it to Agatha. She took it from him with a murmur of thanks, sat down, and began to drink it thirstily. Maddie watched her crossly and then said, 'Out with it, Agatha.'

'Mrs Raisin to you.' The glass of water had given Agatha time to improvise. She hadn't prepared a story, thinking that they would surely send Bill to see her.

'I have reason to believe,' she said, 'that Help Our Homeless was a scam and not a properly organized charity.'

'We know that,' said Maddie to Agatha's amazement. 'The police went to close the place down four years ago, but the office was closed and the Gore-Appleton woman had disappeared.'

'Why didn't you tell me?'

'Why should I?' Maddie was barely able to conceal her contempt. 'The trouble with you women who don't work is you're always poking your nose into other people's affairs. You've been told and told to leave matters to the police. I'll tell you something else. I think you were using that phone. Let's just try the call-back number and see what you were up to.'

Agatha thought quickly. Maddie would only get that operator number. But she would ask everyone in the station if anyone had dialled the operator from the number in the interview room and find that no one had. Then, Agatha worried, she would phone the operator and find out what the inquiry had been about. But just at that moment, the phone rang.

145

Maddie picked it up. 'Hello, Bill,' she said crossly. 'Are you back in the building? You're not? You're phoning from outside.' Bill's voice at the other end quacked busily. 'Well, listen to this,' said Maddie. 'Your darling Mrs Raisin is in the interview room and I think she was using this phone and I was about to get the call-back to tell me who it was phoned her, but because you found out I was in the interview room and decided to get through on an outside line, I can't find out now. Why didn't you just let the switchboard put you through?'

The voice quacked again. It was obvious to Agatha that Bill was explaining that whatever he had to say to Maddie he hadn't wanted to be overheard by the switchboard, because Maddie said, 'This is neither the time nor place, and if you want to know the truth, there never *is* going to be a time and place . . . ever. Geddit?'

She slammed the phone down and said to Agatha, 'Get out of here.'

And Agatha went, gladly.

James was too curious about this new information to be angry with Agatha. In fact, he seemed to find her story about the desk and the manufactured faint amusing.

'Roy Silver phoned when you were out,' he said. 'That secretary, Helen Warwick, the one Derrington was having the affair with, is back. I have the address. Want to go up to London today?'

'Can we leave it till tomorrow?' pleaded Agatha. 'I've

got to go to Cheltenham with the awful Hardy woman and sort out the house sale.'

'Are you driving her or is she driving you?'

'Neither. She's meeting me there.'

'Do you want me to come with you in case she tries to put the price up again?'

'She wouldn't!'

'She might. She's a tough customer.'

'I hate her,' said Agatha passionately. 'I hate her almost as much as I hate that Maddie Hurd. What Bill ever saw in her is beyond me. What a bitch! And we've got Basil to check out.'

'You go and see to getting your home back and we'll drive over to Mircester afterwards and see what we can find out about Basil.'

'And there's the husband, Geoffrey Comfort of the Potato Plus. What is Potato Plus anyway?'

'It's a small factory where they put potatoes in plastic bags for the supermarkets. But his home number is in the book. Guess where he lives?'

'Here? Carsely?'

'No, Ashton-le-Walls, same place as the late Miss Purvey. Off you go.'

Agatha found Mrs Hardy waiting for her in the lawyer's office in Montpelier Terrace in Cheltenham.

Agatha had paid £110,000 for the cottage and had sold it to Mrs Hardy for £120,000. Mrs Hardy was asking for

£130,000, a ridiculous price, thought Agatha, now that the market had slumped.

Agatha was about to sign the papers when the price of £150,000 seemed to leap off the page at her.

'What's this?' she snapped.

'The price?' The lawyer smiled. 'Mrs Hardy said that was the price agreed on.'

'What the hell are the pair of you up to?' snarled Agatha. She rounded on the lawyer. 'You agreed to the price of one hundred and thirty thousand on the phone!'

'Well, Mrs Hardy seems to think one hundred and fifty thousand a fair price.'

Agatha gathered up her handbag and gloves. 'You can get stuffed, the pair of you. I'll tell you what my figure is now – one hundred and ten thousand pounds. Take it or leave it.'

She marched out of the office.

Oh, my home, she mourned as she got in her car. I'd better give it up. I'd better find another cottage in another village and get away from James entirely and get my life back. The world is full of other men.

But when she walked into James's cottage and he looked up and smiled at her, she felt her heart turn over and wondered if she would ever really be free of the feelings she had for him.

She told him what had happened and James said mildly, 'There are other cottages, you know. Let's have an early dinner and go to Mircester.'

* * *

The Loanings, where Basil Morton lived, was a builder's development, rather like the one where the Wong family had their house. It was like a council estate, the only difference that Agatha could see being that the houses were slightly larger and the gardens well tended.

They rang the doorbell, not expecting a reply, but using it as a preliminary to calling on the neighbours and asking where their 'friend', Basil, had got to. To their surprise, the door was answered by a thin, dark-haired woman. At first they thought she was a girl because she was wearing a short navy skirt and white blouse, almost like a school uniform, and her hair was braided into two plaits. But when she switched on the light over the door, they saw the fine wrinkles around her eyes and judged her to be in her late thirties.

'May we speak to Mr Morton?' asked James.

'Basil's away abroad on business. He's often away.' Loneliness shone in the dark eyes. 'Won't you come in?'

They followed her into a living-room, which was almost frightening in its sterile cleanliness. There were no books or magazines lying about. 'How long have you lived here?' asked Agatha, looking around her.

'Ten years.'

And not a scuff-mark or stain or wear anywhere, marvelled Agatha. Can't be any children.

'Sherry?'

'Yes, please.'

'Then please sit down.'

She knelt down in front of a sideboard which shone and gleamed from frequent polishing and took out a crystal decanter, then three crystal glasses and a small silver tray. She put the tray on the carpet and placed the glasses and decanter on it.

'Allow me.' James carried the tray and its contents to a low coffee table, which also shone and gleamed like glass.

How terrifying, thought Agatha. Doesn't she ever spill anything?

The woman poured three glasses of what turned out to be very sweet sherry, probably British sherry, thought James, wrinkling his nose as he sniffed it.

'Did you want to see Basil about business?'

'No, Mrs ... er ... Morton?'

'That's me.'

'We just wanted to talk to him about a personal matter,' said James.

'He's gone abroad. Spain. He often travels.'

'What is his business, Mrs Morton?'

'Bathrooms. Morton's Bathrooms, that's the company.'

'Why Spain?'

'He buys tiles there,' she said vaguely. 'To be honest, I don't really know anything about the business. I have so much to do here, and I'm so tired when Basil gets home that I usually fall asleep.'

'Do you work at home?' asked James.

She gave a little laugh and one thin hand waved to

take in the gleaming living-room. 'Housekeeping. It never ends. You must find that, Mrs . . .?'

'Call me Agatha. I get a woman to clean. I'm not very good at housekeeping.'

'Oh, but you've got to keep on top of it. It's the least one can do for a hard-working husband. I like my Basil to have his little nest to come home to . . . when he does come home,' she added wistfully.

James drained his glass with a little grimace and signalled with his eyes to Agatha.

'Well, we must be on our way, Mrs Morton. We have other calls to make.'

'Oh, must you go? Just a little more sherry?'

'No, really. You're very kind.'

'Who shall I say called?'

'Mr and Mrs Perth.'

'And what else could we ask?' said James as they drove off. 'We could hardly tell that poor neurotic house-cleaner that her husband has gone off to Spain with another woman.'

'What now?' asked Agatha.

'Mr Comfort, I think. Ashton-le-Walls again, and wouldn't you know it. The fog is back.'

'Are we going to tell this Mr Comfort our real names?'

'Yes, I think so.'

'Why did we waste time going to see Basil?'

'Well, we didn't go to see him because we know he's out of the country. I was going to ask the neighbours about him. Funny, I didn't think for a moment that he would be married.'

'I suppose if we had been kind, we should have broken it to her,' said Agatha slowly. 'I think the police will check up and they'll tell her. Oh dear, all that cleaning and polishing in the name of love. He's probably spitting on the floor of his hotel room and leaving rings from his wineglasses on the bedside table.'

'Just look at that bloody fog.' James rubbed at the windscreen with a gloved hand. They had left the dual carriageway and were inching through the fog towards Ashton-le-Walls.

'What are we going to ask him? Oh, look out!' screamed Agatha as a badger loomed up in the headlights. James braked and the badger shambled off into the hedge.

'I don't know,' said James testily. 'For God's sake.' He had moved off again, only to brake savagely once more as a deer leaped through the fog in front of them. 'Why don't those bloody animals stay warm and comfortable instead of wandering about on a filthy night like this? Mr Comfort? We'll play it by ear. He may not even be home. Or we may find ourselves faced with the second Mrs Comfort.'

Geoffrey Comfort lived in a large manor house on the outskirts of the village. 'You'd never think there was all that amount of money in putting potatoes in plastic bags,' marvelled Agatha. 'I'm beginning to think I've spent my life in the wrong trade.'

'Place looks deserted,' muttered James, peering through the fog. 'No, wait a bit. There's a chink of light through the downstairs curtains.'

They parked the car and approached the house and rang the bell.

They waited and waited. 'Probably left the light on because of burglars,' Agatha was beginning, when the door suddenly opened and a middle-aged man stood there, peering at them. He was very fat and round, rather like a potato himself, one of those potatoes washed and bagged for the supermarkets. To add to the impression, his fat face was lightly tanned and he had two black moles on his face, like the eyes of a potato.

'Yes?'

'Mr Comfort?'

'Yes.'

'I am James Lacey and this is Mrs Agatha Raisin.'

'So?'

'Mrs Raisin's husband was murdered recently. He stayed at a health farm at the same time as your wife.'

'Fuck off!' The heavy door was slammed in their faces.

'What do we do now?' asked Agatha.

'We go to the nearest pub and eat and drink, that's what we do. We can't very well ring the bell again and demand he speaks to us.'

A window opened and Mr Comfort's round head appeared. 'And bugger off fast or I'll let the dog out.'

'There's your answer. In the car, quick, Agatha.'

They sped off, James swerving in the drive to avoid a pheasant. 'What's that stupid bird doing awake? Why isn't it up in the trees with the rest of the birds? Why has the whole damned countryside turned suicidal?'

'I could do with a bucket of gin,' said Agatha gloomily. 'Pity you're driving.'

'Never mind. I'll drink just short of any breathalyser test. I'm more interested in food.'

They found the village pub, called quaintly the Tapestry Arms. A menu was chalked up on a blackboard beside the bar. James read it aloud. 'Jumbo sausage and chips, curried chicken and chips, lasagne and chips, fish and chips, and ploughman's.'

'Should we try somewhere else?'

'Not in this fog. Let's try a couple of ploughman's and hope for the best.'

The ploughman's turned out to be rather dry French bread with a minuscule runny pat of butter and a wedge of Cheddar-type cheese which looked for all the world like an old-fashioned slab of carbolic soap.

Agatha's gin and tonic was warm, the pub having run out of ice.

Bands of fog lay across the room. Agatha thrust away her half-eaten food and lit a cigarette. 'Don't glare at me, James. With all this fog about, my cigarette smoke won't make much difference.'

'So you think the Hardy woman will accept your offer?' he asked.

'No, I don't. I think I'm going to have to pay her what she wants. I know it's silly and I know I could get somewhere else quite close, but I want my own place. Did you notice the garden when we were going into her place? Weeds everywhere. Why do people live in the countryside if they don't like living things?' demanded Agatha piously. She wrinkled her nose at her warm gin and tipped it into a rubber plant which was standing on a shelf near her table.

'I gather you don't want to try another of those?'

'No, thank you. And I don't like warm beer either.'

'Then we may as well face a foggy journey home.'

They went outside. The fog had lifted and a fresh wind was blowing. A little moon raced through the clouds above their heads. A shower of beech nuts fell on Agatha's head. 'More nuts!'

'They're poisonous,' said James. 'Poisonous to sheep and cattle. Don't seem to affect the squirrels.'

When they reached home, James said wearily, 'I feel we are going round and round and not getting anywhere. The police have all the resources – to check histories, alibis and bank accounts. Do you think it is really worth going to London tomorrow to see this secretary?'

'Of course.' Agatha was now frightened that if they stopped their investigations, James would take off for foreign parts again. 'You'll feel better about it all in the morning.'

* * *

Helen Warwick was not at the Houses of Parliament but at her flat in a Victorian block in Gloucester Road in Kensington. When she answered the door, Agatha could not believe at first that this lady could have been Sir Desmond's mistress. She was plump and placid, with light grey eyes and brown hair worn in an old-fashioned French pleat. She was wearing a tailored silk blouse and tweed skirt, sensible brogues, and no make-up. James judged her to be in her forties.

James explained, correctly this time, who they were and why they had come. 'You'd better come in,' she said.

The flat was large, rather dark, but very comfortable, with a fire burning brightly in the living-room. There was a large bowl of autumn leaves and chrysanthemums on a polished table by the window. The sofa and chairs had feather cushions. A good Victorian English land-scape hung over the fireplace. It looked as if Miss Warwick had money and had probably always been well off.

'I was shocked when I learned of Desmond's death,' said Helen. 'We were great friends. He was always so kind and courteous. I'm sorry his wife had to find out in such a dreadful way. What's all this about blackmail?'

So they told her all about Jimmy Raisin and Mrs Gore-Appleton. 'I remember them,' said Helen. 'No, they didn't try to blackmail me. I'm the sort that would have gone straight to the police and they probably knew that. I didn't like them one bit. How they found out my real identity I do not know.'

'They probably looked in your handbag,' said Agatha.

'And saw the different name on my credit cards? I suppose so. Horrible people. In fact, now that I come to think of it, I can almost pinpoint the day they found out.'

'Tell us about them,' said Agatha eagerly. 'Everyone else we've asked seems vague, even someone who slept with Jimmy.'

'Let me see . . . would you both like coffee?'

'No, thank you,' said James, anxious to hear what she had to say and frightened that if she went into the kitchen, she might change her mind about talking to them.

'Desmond and I joked about health farms at first. We weren't really interested in our health. We thought it might be an amusing place to get together. His wife might have found a visit to a hotel suspicious but Desmond had told her he was worried about his blood pressure. Jimmy Raisin was a wreck. We arrived on the same day. He was still stinking of booze, but after only a couple of days, he looked like a changed man. He was always oiling around us, my-ladying me to death and claiming to know all sorts of celebrities. He was the sort of man who calls celebs by their first name. He kept talking about his good friend, Tony, who had won an Oscar, and it turned out to be Anthony Hopkins. I don't suppose he even knew him. Mrs Gore-Appleton was not much better. She was – what is it the Americans say? – in my face. She had an abrasive manner overlaid with syrup. You know, she paid me effusive compliments

157

while all the time her sharp eyes watched me to see if I was swallowing any of it. Desmond finally told them we wanted some time to ourselves. The day after that – that would be about five days after we arrived – they began to throw us very *knowing* looks and then pass our table and give contemptuous laughs. I thought it was because Desmond had snubbed them. But they must have found out I wasn't Lady Derrington. What else can I tell you? I thought Jimmy Raisin was a wide boy, what they used to call a spiv. There was something seedy about him. I gathered from the newspapers that you had not seen him in a very long time, Mrs Raisin. The Gore-Appleton woman was blonde and muscular, tried to be very pukka, but there was something all wrong about her. I tell you what. Let me get us all some coffee and I'll think some more.'

Agatha and James waited until she returned with a tray. There was not only coffee but home-made toasted tea-cakes. 'Did you really make these yourself?' James took another appreciative bite. 'These are excellent and the coffee is divine.' He stretched out his long legs. 'It's very comfortable here.'

·Helen gave him a slow smile. 'Come when you're in town and have a free hour to spare.'

Agatha stiffened. This wretched woman suddenly seemed like more competition than any blonde sylph. She was anxious to get James away.

But Helen was talking again. 'You say he slept with some woman?' She laughed. 'I love that euphemism, "slept with". One does anything but.' She gave a warm creamy laugh and Agatha's bearlike eyes fastened on her with barely concealed hate.

'That would be a Mrs Comfort, am I right?'

'How did you know?' said James.

'Oh, he was making up to her and the Gore-Appleton woman was egging him on. I heard him say, "I'll get her tonight," and Mrs Gore-Appleton laughed and said, "Have fun," and the next morning, well, body language and all that, you know what I mean, don't you, James?'

'Oh, absolutely.'

I'll kill this bitch, thought Agatha.

'And that poor spinster lady, she was murdered,' said Helen with an artistic shudder. 'More coffee, James?'

Her tailored silk blouse had a deep V and she leaned forward, deliberately, Agatha thought, to reach for the coffee pot at such an angle that James could see two excellent breasts encased in a frilly brassiere.

James had another full cup of coffee and was helping himself to another tea-cake. Agatha groaned inwardly.

Helen suddenly looked at her. 'I remember now. You and Mr Lacey here were to be married but Jimmy turned up at your wedding.' She laughed again. 'That must have been quite a scene. You'll be able to marry now.'

'Yes,' said Agatha.

'We haven't made any plans,' said James.

There was an awkward silence.

'We should go,' said Agatha harshly.

'Could you just wait until I finish my coffee, *dear*?'

159

Agatha, who had half-risen, sat down again.

'Lacey, Lacey,' Helen was saying. 'Are you any relative of Major-General Robert Lacey?'

'My father. He died some time ago.'

'Oh, then you must know ...' And what followed was the sort of conversation Agatha dreaded, James and Helen animatedly talking about people she did not know.

At last, when Agatha felt she could not stand another moment without screaming, James got to his feet with obvious reluctance.

They took their leave, Agatha first, muttering a grumpy thanks, James after her, stopping to kiss Helen on the cheek and promising to see her again, giving her his card and taking one of hers.

Agatha fumed the whole way back to Carsely. She complained bitterly about harpies who sponged off men instead of going out to work. James tried to point out that as a secretary to a Member of Parliament, Helen did go out to work, but that only seemed to make Agatha worse. He left her at the cottage, saying he had to see someone, whereupon Agatha tortured herself with mad jealousy, imagining him driving back to London to spend the night with Helen. She finally went to bed and tried to read, listening all the while for the sound of his key in the door. At last, just after midnight, she heard him return, heard him come upstairs and go into the bathroom, heard him wash, heard him go to his own room

160

without coming in to say goodnight to her, although he could surely see the light shining under her door.

She raised her head and banged her pillow with her fist, put out the light, and tried to compose herself for sleep. But sleep would not come as she tossed and turned, tormenting herself with pictures of a world out there full of women all too ready to snatch James away from her.

And then she stiffened. She heard a furtive noise from somewhere downstairs and then the clack of the letterbox, then a sound like water being poured. She pulled on her dressing-gown and ran down the stairs. She opened the door to the hall as a gloved hand threw a lighted match through the letterbox. In that instant Agatha leaped back into the living-room and screamed, 'James!' just as a sheet of flame reached out for her.

He came hurtling down the stairs. 'We're on fire,' shouted Agatha. She made to open the door again but he pulled her back.

'Go up to the bathroom and pour buckets of water on the floor. It's over the hall. We've got to stop the fire getting to the thatch!'

James ran to the kitchen as Agatha scampered up the stairs. Swearing, he filled a bucket of water and running back with it, hurled the contents at the living-room door, which was already beginning to blister and crackle.

Upstairs, Agatha, sobbing with fright, poured water on the bathroom floor. There were shouts and yells from outside. Agatha clearly heard the voice of the pub landlord, John Fletcher, calling, 'Keep throwing that earth. We daren't wait for the fire brigade. Oh, Mrs Hardy. More earth. Let's be having it! That there's a petrol fire. I can smell it.'

Then, just as James shouted up, 'It's all right now, Agatha,' she heard the sirens of police cars and the fire engine in the distance. She went slowly down the stairs and sat on the bottom steps with her head in her hands.

The living-room door now stood open to reveal the black and smouldering wreck of the little hall, piled high with a mound of earth.

'Who would do a thing like this?' demanded James. 'Someone meant to roast us alive.'

'Probably Helen Warwick,' said Agatha, and she burst into tears.

Chapter Seven

Suddenly the house seemed to be full of people.

Fred Griggs, the policeman; Mrs Bloxby, with a sweater and trousers pulled on over her pyjamas; John Fletcher, the publican; Mrs Hardy; and various other villagers.

'You've got Mrs Hardy here to thank for quick action,' said Fred. 'She phoned the fire brigade and then ran with buckets of earth to put on the fire. Water don't do much to stop a petrol fire.'

'Are you all right, Mrs Raisin?' Mrs Hardy's normally bad-tempered face registered concern.

'Bit shaken,' said Agatha.

'Who could have done such a thing?'

Agatha shuddered and wrapped her arms closely about herself. 'I just don't know.'

By the time the police arrived and then Bill Wong, and two other detectives Agatha did not know, the Carsely Ladies' Society had commandeered the kitchen and were making tea for all. Agatha was being fussed over and handed home-made cakes. John Fletcher had brought a case of beer along from the pub and was serving out drinks to the men. James was looking around the crowded cottage in a bemused way and wondering whether to put on some music and make a party of it.

But the police cleared everyone out after having heard a report from the fire chief, and the detectives settled down to interview Agatha and James.

'You've been putting that stick of yours in muddy waters and stirring things up,' Bill accused Agatha. 'Who did you go to see today?' He glanced at the clock. 'Or rather, yesterday.'

James flashed Agatha a warning glance, but Agatha said, 'Helen Warwick.'

'What! That secretary who was having an affair with Sir Desmond Derrington? I told you two not to interfere!'

James said wearily, 'I know you did. But until this murder, or murders, is cleared up, Agatha and I feel we will always be suspects.'

'I'll talk to you about that later. Now, who else did you see?'

'No one else yesterday.'

'The day before?'

James hesitated. Then he shrugged and said, 'Mrs Comfort had gone off to Spain with her lover, a Basil Morton who lives in Mircester. We went to see what we could find out about him. He's married and his wife hadn't a clue what he was up to, so we left. Then we went to see Mrs Comfort's ex-husband in Ashton-le-Walls. He threatened to set the dog on us. End of story.'

'And how did you find out about Mr Comfort? His address? Come to think of it, how did you get the addresses of those other people who were at the health farm?'

Agatha said, 'Roy Silver employed a detective to find out about Jimmy. She dug up the addresses for us.'

'Name?'

'Can't remember,' mumbled Agatha.

'We'll ask Silver.'

Agatha looked helplessly at James.

'There's no need to lie, Agatha,' said James. 'We had a short stay at the health farm, Bill, and while we were there, I had a chance to look at the records. Do you think the rest of the questioning could be left until we've had some sleep? We're both rather shaky.'

'All right. But I expect you both at police headquarters as soon as you can manage it.'

As Bill Wong drove off with the others, his first thought was, I've a lot to tell Maddie – followed hard by another thought, I'm damned if I will. It was strange they couldn't find the Gore-Appleton woman. And yet there was something nagging at the back of his mind, something someone had said, something very obvious he hadn't thought of doing.

The village carpenter effected temporary repairs, putting up chipboard and a makeshift door the next day while James phoned the insurance company. Mrs Hardy

165

phoned Agatha and asked if she would 'step next door' for a chat. 'I'll see what she wants, James,' said Agatha, 'and then we'd better get off to Mircester.'

Agatha went reluctantly next door. She had taken such a dislike to Mrs Hardy, and yet the woman had done everything she could to help put out the fire. Not only that, she had saved their lives, thought Agatha. That was a wild exaggeration, when they could both have escaped out of the back door.

But it was a changed Mrs Hardy who answered the door to her. 'Come in, you poor thing,' she said. 'What a nightmare!'

'Thank you for all your efforts on our behalf.' Agatha followed her into the kitchen.

'Coffee?'

'Yes, please.'

Mrs Hardy poured two cups of coffee. They both sat down at the kitchen table.

'I'll come straight to the point.' Mrs Hardy twisted her coffee cup nervously in her ringed hands. 'I decided to settle in the country for peace and quiet. I was finding it all too quiet, but what happened to you last night was frightening, not my idea of excitement. There's a maniac on the loose and I want out of here. I am prepared to take your offer of one hundred and ten thousand pounds.'

Agatha had a sudden impulse to say she would make it one hundred and thirty, the sum she had originally offered, but bit it back in time.

'When do you want to settle at the lawyers'?'

'Today, if possible,' said Mrs Hardy.

'Let me see, we're just about to go into Mircester to make our statements. We could go on from there to Cheltenham. What about four o'clock?'

'I'll fix it.'

'Tell me,' said Agatha curiously, 'what is it about Carsely that you don't like, apart from murder and mayhem?'

She gave a little sigh. 'I've been very lonely since my husband died. I thought a small village would be a friendly place.'

'But it is!' protested Agatha. 'Everyone's prepared to be friendly if you just give them a chance.'

'But it means going to church and talking to the yokels in the pub and joining some dreadful ladies' society.'

'I find them delightful.'

'Well, I don't. I like cities. I'll rent in London. I'll put my stuff in storage and take a service flat for a few weeks and look around.'

But that remark of Mrs Hardy's about not being able to make friends had gone straight to Agatha's heart as she remembered her own lonely days before coming to Carsely.

She said, 'Why don't you stay? We could be friends.'

'That's very kind of you.' Mrs Hardy gave a wry smile. 'Don't you want your cottage back?'

'Well, I do, but . . .'

'Then you shall have it. I'll see you at the lawyers' this afternoon.'

'And that was that,' said Agatha to James a few minutes later. 'So I'll soon be home again. She said as I was leaving that provided all the papers were signed, I can move in in a fortnight.'

James felt slightly irritated. A moment before it had seemed that all he wanted out of life was to have his cottage to himself, without Agatha Raisin dribbling cigarette ash over everything. He decided that she ought to look less delighted at the prospect of leaving his home.

'Well, if you're ready,' he said, 'let's get to police headquarters.'

Leaves fluttered down in front of them as they drove off, autumn leaves, dancing and whirling, blown down by a great gusty wind from a sky full of tumbling black, ragged clouds.

The whole countryside was in motion. Showers of nuts pattered on the roof of the car. A woman getting out of a car at the Quarry Garage clutched at her skirts to hold them down. An old newspaper spiralled up and then performed a hectic dance through the furrows of a brown ploughed field. And somewhere, thought Agatha, crawling around out there is a murderer.

'It must be something to do with that Helen Warwick,' she said.

'Don't be ridiculous,' snapped James. 'Do you mean

she travelled down from London to pour petrol through our letterbox? Why?'

'Because I swear she knows something.'

'Oh, really. Then I had better go back and see her.'

'Yes, you'd like that, wouldn't you?'

'Very much. I found her a charming woman.'

'Men are so blind. She was sly and devious. And mercenary.'

'In your jealous opinion, Agatha.'

'I'm not jealous of that plump frump. We could have been killed last night.'

'Not with a back door to the garden.'

'What if we had both been asleep?'

There was no answer to that.

They completed the drive to Mircester in silence.

There were many questions to answer at police head-quarters. Detective Inspector Wilkes was in charge of the questioning this time, flanked by Bill Wong. Agatha found herself beginning to sweat. She was terrified either she or James would let something slip and Wilkes would know about their burglaring.

When it was at last all over and they had signed their statements, Wilkes said severely, 'I should charge both of you with obstructing police business. But I'm warning you for the last time. We may seem to you very slow, but we are thorough.'

They left feeling chastened. From an upstairs window, Maddie Hurd watched them go. She bit her thumbnail and stared down at them. She had not been invited to join in the interrogation. She had not been asked to do anything further on the case at all. She had been given a series of burglaries to investigate instead. She blamed Bill Wong for turning her superiors against her.

Although Bill had not opened his mouth, her jilting of him had a lot to do with it. Bill Wong was very popular, Maddie was not. Women, even in the police force, were expected to be womanly. Women in the police force were not expected to jilt fellow officers. So, although Chief Inspector Wilkes did not sit down and say, 'We don't want Maddie Hurd on the case because of the way she has treated Bill Wong,' he had, without even thinking about it, decided she was not the right officer for the job.

Agatha completed the business of buying her cottage back, although conscience prompted her finally to offer £120,000. She felt she had misjudged Mrs Hardy, that here was a fellow spirit.

When they were leaving the lawyers', Agatha said impulsively, 'Look, there's a dance at the village hall on Saturday evening. Why don't you come with me and James? No, don't refuse right away. I thought I would hate things like that, but they're really rather fun. And it's in a good cause. We're raising money for Cancer Relief.'

Mrs Hardy gave a weak smile. All her aggression seemed to have left her. 'Well, maybe . . .' she said hesitantly.

'That's the thing. Think about it.' Agatha waved good-bye and headed off to the car, where James was waiting for her.

'Well, that's that,' she said cheerfully. 'Do you know, she's not that bad? I've asked her to come to the dance with us on Saturday.'

James groaned. 'I didn't know we were going.'

'Of course we are. What would a village dance be without us?'

Agatha put on a chiffon evening blouse and black velvet skirt for the dance on Saturday, wishing the days of proper evening gowns even for a village hop were not gone forever. Full evening dress was glamorous. She was regretting her decision to 'mother' Mrs Hardy at the dance. And yet surely there was no one in the village to catch James's wandering eye. And he *did* have a wandering eye, witness his interest in Helen Warwick.

He must have meant something hopeful by that 'Give me time.' Perhaps they could go away together to northern Cyprus just for a holiday. It wouldn't need to be a honeymoon. She sat at her dressing-table, a lipstick halfway to her mouth, her eyes unfocused by dreams as she imagined them walking along the beach together, talking.

Then she gave a shrug and, leaning forward, applied the lipstick with a careful hand. The dream James always talked so well, always said all those delightful things

171

she longed to hear. The real James would probably talk about books or the political situation. She stood up. Her skirt was loose at the waist. No thanks to that brief stay at the health farm. It was a result of living with James and eating James's carefully prepared meals – no fries, no puddings. There was no incentive either to snack before meals because she still felt obliged to ask him for everything, and it was easier not to eat anything between meals than to request something and maybe be damned as a glutton. Her face was thinner and her skin clear. I could pass for forty – maybe, thought Agatha.

When they collected Mrs Hardy and they began to walk towards the village hall, Agatha glanced sideways at her and thought she might at least have made some effort with her dress. Mrs Hardy was wearing a rather baggy green tweed skirt and a black blouse under a raincoat.

'I don't think this is a very good idea,' said Mrs Hardy. 'I don't like dancing.'

'Stay for a bit and have a drink,' urged Agatha, 'and then, if you still don't like it, you can go home.'

Light was streaming out of the village hall and they could hear the jolly umpty-tumpty sound of the village band. 'It'll be old-fashioned dancing tonight, not a disco,' said Agatha. 'No heavy metal.'

'You mean "Pride of Erin" and the military two-step, things like that?'

'Yes.'

'Oh, I can do those,' said Mrs Hardy. 'I didn't know

172

anyone did those sort of dances these days. I thought they just took ecstasy pills and threw themselves about like dervishes.'

They left their coats in the temporary cloakroom manned, or 'womanned', by old Mrs Boggle. 'That'll be fifty pee each,' said Mrs Boggle, 'and hang your own coats up.'

'It's the first time I've ever been charged for a cloakroom ticket at the village hall,' said Agatha suspiciously.

'You don't think I'm going to do this for nothing,' grumbled Mrs Boggle.

James paid the money and then led them both into the village hall. 'The next dance is a Canadian barn dance,' announced the MC, vicar Alf Bloxby.

James turned to Mrs Hardy. 'Care to try?'

'I don't know . . .'

'Oh, go on,' said Agatha, determined to be charitable and reminding herself that she would soon be moving back into her old home.

James and Mrs Hardy took the floor. Agatha moved over to the bar, where the publican, John Fletcher, was working, having left his wife and son to manage the pub. 'Gin and tonic, John,' said Agatha.

'Right you are. How's that murder investigation going? They caught anyone?'

Agatha shook her head.

'It's odd, isn't it? And then the murder of that poor woman in the cinema. Mind you, the police don't think now that the two murders are related.'

'Since when?'

'I dunno. Fred Griggs was saying something like that the other day.'

He turned away to serve someone else.

Agatha found Mrs Bloxby next to her. 'Mrs Hardy appears to have come out of her shell,' said the vicar's wife.

Agatha turned round and surveyed the dance floor. Mrs Hardy was dancing with unexpected grace. She was laughing at something James was saying.

'And if I am not mistaken, that's quite a flirtatious look in her eyes. Not,' added Mrs Bloxby hurriedly, 'that she is any competition. You are looking remarkably trim and well these days.'

'Must be James's cooking,' said Agatha. 'We brought along Mrs Hardy to cheer her up. I only hope now she doesn't cheer up too much or she will decide to stay.'

'But you have your cottage back?'

'Yes, everything's signed and agreed on.'

'In that case, she can do nothing about it.'

'I hope James is not going to get carried away by my good Samaritan act,' said Agatha. 'If he asks her for the next dance, I'll murder her . . . oh, dear, how easily one says things like that. I don't think we're ever going to find out who murdered Jimmy.'

'Let's sit over there in the corner, away from the noise of the band, and you can tell me about it,' said Mrs Bloxby.

Agatha hesitated. The dance had finished. But James was asking Miss Simms for the next dance.

'Okay,' she said. They carried their drinks over to a couple of chairs in a corner of the hall.

'I think a lot of it you already know,' began Agatha. 'Jimmy, and possibly this Mrs Gore-Appleton, who ran a dicey charity, stayed at a health farm, found out what they could, and blackmailed some of the other guests. I believe one of them murdered him.' She went on to describe all their investigations.

Mrs Bloxby listened carefully and then she said, 'I would think the most likely suspect would be Mrs Gore-Appleton herself.'

'But they were in it together!'

'Exactly. Jimmy went back on the booze and down to the gutter. But he surfaced for long enough to get cleaned up for your wedding. So, say, before that he had some stage where he was relatively sober and needed money. Why should he not seek out his old protector? And think of this. Let's say she wants nothing more to do with him – her miraculous cured alcoholic isn't cured. So she tries to send him packing. But Jimmy has a taste for blackmail, and as he was close to her at one time, he must have known about the fraudulent charity. He knows the police are looking for her. So he says something like, "Pay up or I'll tell them where you are"? Wait a bit. It could be just before he came down here. He says he's going to be in Carsely. She follows him and waits for the right moment, and what better moment is

175

there than when he is hopelessly drunk and has just had a row with his wife?'

Agatha looked at her open-mouthed and then said, 'That's all so very simple, it could well be what happened. But surely the police can find this woman, with all their resources.'

'She could have changed her name.'

'That might be an idea. I wonder if they've checked the Records Office to see if a Mrs Gore-Appleton changed her name to anything else. Damn, they're bound to have done that.'

'She was and still is a criminal, Agatha. She could easily get false papers. Apart from her, have you come across anyone during your investigations who might be a murderer or murderess?'

'It could be any of them. Those men's footprints near the body could be a blind. I have a gut feeling it's some woman. That secretary, Helen Warwick, I don't trust her at all.'

'It would take some strength to strangle a man.'

'Mrs Comfort said something odd about Mrs Gore-Appleton. She said she looked like a man.'

'So she could be a he, pretending to be a woman?'

'I suppose anything's possible.'

'There you are,' said James. 'Dance, Agatha?'

'Sit down a moment,' said Agatha. 'Mrs Bloxby's got some ideas.' By the time Mrs Bloxby had finished outlining them, her husband was announcing a ladies' choice, and to Agatha's dismay, Mrs Hardy came up and

176

tapped James on the shoulder and marched him off rather like a military policeman arresting a deserter.

'I wish that woman would go back in her shell,' muttered Agatha. She was beginning to have that old feeling of being a wallflower. Then she remembered it was a ladies' choice and asked one of the farmers for a dance.

Mrs Bloxby watched her and reflected that Agatha was looking almost pretty. Her eyes were too small and her figure, however slimmed down, always appeared a bit stocky, but she had excellent legs and her brown hair shone with health.

Agatha began to forget about murder and enjoyed the evening. James asked her for the next dance and then they moved to the bar for some companionable drinks. Mrs Hardy was on her feet for every dance, her face flushed, her eyes shining.

'Who would have thought that nasty old bat would turn out to be so nice, if you know what I mean,' said Agatha.

The village dance ended as usual at midnight. They said their goodnights, Agatha noticing that old Mrs Boggle, having collected the money, had cleared off, leaving all the coats unguarded.

They walked home, Mrs Hardy hanging on to James's arm, much to Agatha's irritation, and saying what a good evening it had been. They were just rounding the corner of Lilac Lane when a dark figure detached itself from the thicker blackness of the bushes.

In the dim light from the moon above, they saw with horror that a man was confronting them, a masked man who was holding a pistol.

'This is a warning,' he grated. 'Bugger off. And just to make sure you know I mean business . . .'

The pistol was lowered to point at Agatha's legs.

For one split second they stood paralysed, then Mrs Hardy's foot shot out like that of a karate expert and she kicked the gun out of the man's hand. He turned and fled. Mrs Hardy went plunging after him, but tripped and fell headlong, blocking James's pursuit. He tripped over her and sprawled in the lane.

Agatha found her voice and began to scream for help.

More police interviews. Agatha, white and shaking, was somehow more upset to learn that the gun was a replica. Mrs Hardy was told she had been very brave but very foolish. It could have been a real gun.

'Where did you learn to kick like that?' asked Bill Wong.

Mrs Hardy laughed. 'From those kung fu films on television. I suppose it was a silly thing to do – it was just an accident that I managed to kick the gun out of his hand.'

'Remember,' cautioned Bill, 'that if that gun had been real and had been loaded, it could have gone off.'

'Well, I think she was very brave,' said Agatha, clutching a cup of hot sweet tea.

While James and Mrs Hardy were being questioned again – what had the man's voice sounded like, what height, clothes? – Agatha began to think of Helen Warwick. They had gone to see Helen and then James's house had been set on fire, and now this.

There must be some connection.

But when the police had left to join the milling hordes of other police combing the area – armed police, police with dogs, and police with helicopters – and when Mrs Hardy had finally gone to her cottage, Agatha broached her suspicions of Helen Warwick to James. He shrugged and said, 'That's ridiculous.'

'It's not ridiculous!' cried Agatha.

'You've had a bad fright,' said James soothingly. 'I've got to go to London tomorrow to see an old friend. I suggest you have a day in bed to recover. No, not another word. You're not in a fit state to think properly.'

Agatha awoke at nine to find the cottage empty and James's car gone. She was suddenly angry. Damn it, she would go to London herself and ask Roy Silver if he had found out anything else from that detective.

The doorbell rang. She ran to answer it, hoping James had come back. But it was the vicar's wife who stood on the step.

'Oh, Mrs Bloxby. Come in. I was just about to leave for London.'

'I keep telling you to call me Margaret. And shouldn't you be resting?'

'Have they caught anyone?' asked Agatha over her shoulder as she led the way through to the kitchen.

'Not a sign. They're still searching. The woods above the village are full of men and dogs. Was the man wearing gloves?'

'I think so. Why?'

'Well, fingerprints.'

Agatha seized the coffee jug from the machine. Her hand suddenly shook and she dropped the coffee jug, which did not break but bounced across the floor, spreading coffee and spattering the cupboards. Agatha burst into tears.

'Now, then,' said Mrs Bloxby, guiding her to the table. 'You just sit down there and I'll clean up this mess.'

'J-James is so-so pernickety,' sobbed Agatha. 'He'll be furious.'

'By the time I've finished,' said the vicar's wife, taking off her coat, 'he won't know anything has happened.'

She opened the cupboard under the sink and took out cleaning materials and a floor-cloth. While Agatha sniffed dismally into a handkerchief, Mrs Bloxby worked calmly and efficiently. Then she put on the kettle, saying, 'I think tea would be better for you. Your nerves are bad enough. I am surprised James has left. Why?'

'He said he had to see an old friend.' Agatha, who had temporarily got a grip on herself, found she was beginning to cry again. 'But I don't think he's gone to see any old friend, I think he's gone to see that murderess, Helen Warwick.'

'I'll make us a cup of tea and you can tell me about it.'

When they were both seated at the table, Agatha described the visit to Helen Warwick and how, after that visit, someone had tried to burn them to death, and then, last night, the masked man had been about to shoot her in the legs if Mrs Hardy had not kicked the gun out of his hand.

'I heard about that last night. Very brave of Mrs Hardy. But it all goes to show, Agatha, that your Christian act in taking her to the village dance had its reward. It always reinforces my belief in the fundamental goodness of people in the way that a little bit of kindness engenders such a reward.'

Agatha managed a watery smile. 'Doesn't seem to work with the Boggles.'

'Oh, them, well ... There is always an exception. But surely James's interest in Helen Warwick is simply to do with the case?'

'James has quite dreadful taste in women,' said Agatha gloomily. 'Remember Mary Fortune?' Mary Fortune, a divorcée who had been murdered, had enjoyed a brief affair with James before her death.

'You were away then,' pointed out Mrs Bloxby. 'Have there been any reporters, asking questions?'

'About the attempted shooting? No. I think the police want the press out of their hair and they have somehow

181

managed to keep it quiet for the moment. The villagers are tired of the press as well, so none of them is going to phone up a newspaper. I'll go to London and see if Roy Silver has found out anything. I've something in mind. I may stay the night. I'd best leave a note for James.'

'Hadn't you better stick around? The police will surely be back to see you.'

'They can talk to the Hardy woman. I want a change of scene anyway.'

'I do feel you should take care, Agatha. Someone appears to be more afraid of your investigations than they are of the police.'

'I'm beginning to think that someone is mad. Look, it was a man who held us up last night. Mrs Comfort said something about Mrs Gore-Appleton looking like a man. Perhaps there never was a Mrs Gore-Appleton. Perhaps there was a Mr Gore-Appleton. Perhaps some man pretended to be a woman as part of that charity scam.'

'I still think you should stay here and rest, Agatha.'

'No, I'm going. I'll feel better once I'm out of the village.' But Agatha forgot to leave a note for James.

Once she reached London, Agatha found herself driving towards Kensington, to Gloucester Road. She had to reassure herself that James had really gone to see a friend and that the friend wasn't Helen Warwick. As she drove along Gloucester Road towards the block of flats, she kept looking at the parked cars. Of course, James could be parked anywhere. It was difficult to find a parking place in Kensington at the best of times. His car could be tucked away in Cornwall Gardens or Emperor's Gate or somewhere she could not see it. But suddenly, there it was, on a meter, a few yards from Helen's building. And as a final nail in Agatha's coffin, there, just leaving the flats, came James and Helen, laughing and talking like old friends. The car behind Agatha, who had been driving at about five miles an hour, hooted impatiently. Agatha speeded up. She longed to turn the car around, catch up with them and hurl abuse at James from the window.

But she drove along Palace Gate instead, made a left at Kensington Gardens and headed over to the City.

Roy was in his office. He backed away behind his desk when he saw the grim look on Agatha's face. 'What have you been up to, sweetie?'

Agatha told him all about the fire, the attempted shooting, and their investigations. Roy visibly relaxed, assuming that all this mayhem was the reason for Agatha's angry face and not anything to do with himself.

'Perhaps it's that Hardy woman after all,' he said when Agatha had finished. 'She turned up out of nowhere to live in Carsely. What if she's really Mrs Gore-Appleton? I mean, coincidences happen the whole time. Lots of people move to the Cotswolds and find them-selves living next to someone they've been trying to avoid all their lives. So how's this? She takes your cottage. The fact that your name is Raisin and you're probably Jimmy's wife amuses her. It's not all that usual a name. She knows about your proposed wedding to James but thinks you must be divorced. Jimmy may not even have mentioned you. Then, in his fumbling, drunken wanderings, he runs into her, recognizes her as his old buddy and tries to put the screws on her. She bumps him off. Then she goes to that cinema in Mircester and there, in the cinema, she sees Miss Purvey and, what is worse, Miss Purvey sees her, so Miss Purvey must be silenced . . .

'Now she's running scared. She tries to burn the pair of you to death, but some neighbour starts screaming, "Fire!" and she sees your light upstairs and hears you shouting, "James!" or something and decides, as you are not going to die, she'd better start heaving buckets of earth around to make sure she's not suspected. Then she thinks up a scheme to throw you off the scent. She hires some actor or villain to stage that hold-up and give you a fright and at the same time she can figure as the heroine of the piece, and who's going to suspect a heroine?'

'That's very clever, Roy, and I wish it could stand up, but the fact is James and I went into her cottage – I've still got the keys – and we went through her papers and she is exactly who she says she is.'

'Damn.'

184

'Your detective seems to have a touch with the down-and-outs that the police lack.'

'The problem with Iris is that she's very busy at the moment. She's overworked. She's got at least a couple of battered wives on her books.'

'See if you can get her. I'll pay her.' Agatha walked to the window and stared out unseeing at the jumble of City roofs and spires.

Then she swung round. 'I know, we'll go and see what we can find out.'

'We, Paleface? I've a job to do here, remember?'

The door opened and Bunty, Agatha's former secretary, popped her head round the door. 'Oh, hello, Mrs R. Roy, Mr Wilson wants to see you.'

'I'll wait for you,' said Agatha.

Roy went off, straightening his garish tie and wondering whether it was *too* gaudy for a rising young executive.

Mr Wilson surveyed Roy for a few moments and then said, 'You've got the Raisin woman there.'

'Just dropped by for a chat.'

'That one never drops by for a chat. What does she want? To wring your neck for having buggered up her love-life?'

'No, she wants my help. She's crazy. She wants us to go among the down-and-outs and find out more about her husband's background.'

'Then do it.'

'What?'

'I said, do it. Agatha Raisin may be the nastiest, most

ball-breaking woman I have ever come across, but she's the best PR in the business and I would like her on the payroll. I want you to be very nice to her. I want you to point out to her that since she retired, her life has been nothing but stress and murder down in that village. Hint that there's a good amount of money to be made. Put her in your debt.'

'But I've got a meeting with Allied Soaps this afternoon.'

'Patterson can take that. Off with you, and keep the old girl sweet.'

Roy trailed miserably back to his office. Allied Soaps was an important account and Patterson would dearly like to get his hands on it. Life just wasn't fair.

He opened the door of his office and pinned a resolute smile on his face. 'Guess what? I've got a slow day, so we can go.'

Agatha looked at him suspiciously. 'What did Wilson want with you? Not trying to get me back on the payroll?'

'No, no.' Roy knew that if he told Agatha that was the only reason he was going to help her, it would alienate her for all time.

'Well, we'd better get some old clothes and look the part.'

'Do we have to dress up?'

'Don't worry. I'll go and find the right stuff. See you back here in about an hour.'

* * *

Some time later, two shabby individuals stood outside Pedmans in Cheapside and tried to flag down a cab. Agatha had gone to an Oxfam shop for the clothes they were now wearing. Roy was dressed in jeans which Agatha had ripped at the knees for him, a denim shirt and an old tweed jacket. Agatha was wearing a long floral skirt and two lumpy cardigans over a blouse and carrying various plastic bags. Both stank of methylated spirits, Agatha having doused their clothes liberally in the stuff. She had also dirtied their faces.

'This is no good,' said Roy as the third empty cab sailed by them without stopping. Agatha went back into Pedmans and hailed the commissionaire.

'What d'ye want?' he growled.

'It's me, Agatha Raisin,' she snapped. 'Get out there and find a cab for me.'

The commissionaire, who loathed Agatha, stared down at her, a smile breaking across his face. So the old bag had fallen on hard times. Let her find her own bloody cab.

'Shove off,' he said. 'We don't want the likes of you in here.'

Agatha opened her mouth to blast him, but a quiet voice behind the commissionaire said, 'Jock, get Mrs Raisin a cab, and hop to it.'

Mr Wilson stood there. 'Going off to a fancy dress party, Mrs Raisin?'

'That's it,' said Agatha.

Jock ran out into the street and flagged down a cab, and with his face averted held the door open for Agatha and Roy. Agatha pressed something into his hand. He touched his hat. The cab rolled off. Jock opened his hand. A penny! He hurled it into the gutter and stumped back inside.

'You haven't brought your handbag?' asked Roy.

'No, I left it with your secretary. It's in her desk. You left your wallet, I hope?'

'Yes, but who's paying for this cab?'

'You are!'

'But I left all my money behind!'

'So did I. I mean, I've got about a pound in change, but that won't pay for this cab to Waterloo.'

'What are we going to do?' wailed Roy. 'Of all the stupid—'

'Let's just hope it's not one of those cabs where they lock the doors.' The cab slowed and stopped at traffic lights.

'Now!' said Agatha.

She wrenched open the door and, followed by Roy, dived out into the street, pursued by the outraged howls of the cabby.

'You can still run,' panted Roy when they finally came to a halt.

Agatha clutched her side. 'I've got a pain. I really must get back into condition.'

They started to walk, an aroma of methylated spirits floating out from them. 'I think we had better do some

188

begging,' said Agatha, stopping in the middle of London Bridge.

'We don't look appealing enough. We need a dog or a child.'

'We haven't got one. Can't you sing or something?'

'Nobody would hear a note with this traffic noise. Beggars who get money are either pathetic or threatening.'

'Okay.' Agatha stepped in front of a businessman and held out her hand. 'Money for food,' she said. 'Or else.'

He stopped and looked her up and down.

'Or else what?'

'Or else I'll hit you with my bottle.'

'Get lost, or I'll call the police, you scum. It's layabouts like you that are bringing this country to its knees. You're too old to work, but you should get your son to support you.'

Roy giggled maliciously.

The businessman appealed to the passers-by. 'Can you believe this? They're demanding money with menaces.'

'Come on, Aggie,' pleaded Roy, getting frightened, as a crowd started to collect.

'Police!' a woman started to shout. 'Police!'

They took to their heels again, thumping their way over the bridge until they had left the crowd behind.

'All this running, birdbrain,' snarled Agatha. 'We should have run back to the office and got some money.'

'Not far now,' said Roy. 'Let's get it over with.'

Dusk was falling. The roar of the going-home traffic drummed in their ears. Agatha thought of James and wondered what he was doing.

James was feeling guilty. He had taken Helen Warwick out for lunch and then gone back to her flat at her suggestion for coffee. She had a day off, she had explained. Life was quiet when the House wasn't sitting.

Perhaps because she had really nothing more to tell him than she had already told, perhaps because she did not seem nearly as charming as she had when he had first met her, James was able to realize that this visit had been prompted more by a desire not to let Agatha dominate his life than by any real interest in Helen. She was very clever at extracting information, and the information she seemed most interested in was the size of his bank balance. No question was direct or vulgar. Talk of stocks and shares, whether he had suffered over the Lloyd's or Barings disasters, things like that. And the friends they were supposed to have in common began to seem to James like people she had met at parties and in the course of her work but did not really know very well.

'Do you mind if I make a telephone call?' he said at last. 'And then I really must go.'

'Help yourself.'

He dialled home and let it ring for a long time.

190

'No reply,' he said with a rueful smile.

'Were you trying to get Mrs Raisin?'

'Yes.'

'Oh, she's in town.'

'How do you know that?'

'I saw her driving past when we walked out for lunch.'

'Why didn't you say anything?'

'I was just about to, but you were talking about something and then the whole matter slipped my mind.'

Now James felt like a guilty husband who had been caught out in an adulterous act. He then became angry because he was sure Agatha had come to town for no other purpose but to spy on him.

'I'd better go. Thanks for the coffee.'

'Oh, do stay,' said Helen. 'I've nothing planned for this evening.'

'I'm afraid I have.'

She stood up and moved close to him. He moved back and found his legs pressed against the sofa. She raised her arms to put them around his neck, a slow seductive smile on her face. James ducked, stepped up on the sofa and walked over the back, his long legs taking him straight to the door.

'Goodbye,' he said, opened the door and ran down the stairs.

'Silly old fool,' he said aloud, but he meant himself and not Agatha Raisin.

* * *

Agatha had had the foresight to buy two bottles of cheap sweet wine called Irish Blossom. They were the kind of wine bottles with screw-tops rather than corks. She and Roy found a group of down-and-outs near where Jimmy Raisin used to hang out. They were a mixed bunch, but more solid alcoholics than drug addicts, the drug addicts being younger and favouring better sites. The Celtic races predominated, Scottish and Irish, making Agatha wonder if there was any truth in the statement that alcoholism got worse the farther north in the world one went.

No one seemed to want to know them, until Agatha fished in one of her plastic bags and produced a bottle of wine.

The others gathered around. Roy passed the bottle round. The contents were soon gone. An old man came up. He had two bottles of cider, which he proceeded to share. He had an educated voice and told everyone he used to be a professor. Soon they all began to talk, and Agatha and Roy found they were surrounded by jet pilots, famous footballers, brain surgeons and tycoons. 'It's a bit like those people who believe they had a previous life,' muttered Agatha. 'They were always Napoleon or Cleopatra or someone like that.'

'They believe what they're saying,' whispered Roy. 'They've told the same lies so many times, they actually believe them now.'

Agatha raised her voice. 'We had a mate used to hang around about here,' she said. 'Jimmy Raisin.'

The man with the educated voice, who was called Charles, said, 'Someone said he got killed. Good riddance, sleazy little toe-rag.'

They must have heard about the murder by word of mouth, thought Agatha. Few of them would ever look at a newspaper.

'What happened to his stuff?' asked Roy.

'Perlice took it away,' said a thin woman with the avid face and glittering eyes of a Hogarth drawing. 'Took 'is box and all. But Lizzie got 'is bag o'stuff.'

'What stuff?' Roy's voice was sharp.

'Just who the hell are you?' asked Charles.

Agatha glared at Roy. 'I'll tell you who I am,' he said, his voice slightly slurred. 'I'm a big executive in the City. I only come down here evenings because I like the company.'

There was a general easing of tension as the brain surgeons, jet pilots and tycoons in general regarded what they thought was one of their own kind. 'And I'll tell you something more.' Roy fished in the capacious inside pocket of his Oxfam jacket. 'I took this bottle of Scotch out of the desk before I came here.'

This was nothing but the truth, but deep in the dim recesses of their brains they accepted him as a fellow liar. The Scotch was passed round. Since they were all, with the exception of Agatha and Roy, topping up from the last binge, it had the effect of knocking them into almost immediate drunkenness.

193

Agatha found the avid-faced woman was called Clara and sidled over to her. 'Tell you a secret,' she whispered.

Clara looked at her, her glittering eyes slightly unfocused. 'I was married to Jimmy,' said Agatha.

'Go on!'

'Fact. So that bag this Lizzie took belongs to me. Where is she?'

'She'll be along.'

So Agatha and Roy settled themselves to wait. More joined them. More cheap drink. A man built a bonfire in an old oil drum. Clara began to sing drunkenly.

It was an almost seductive way of life, thought Agatha, provided the weather wasn't too cold. Just chuck up reality, goodbye to work, to family, to responsibility, beg during the day and get stoned out of your mind at night. No conventions to bind you, no getting or spending, no hassle.

'I wash not allush like thish,' slurred Charles at one point. 'I wash a profeshor at Oxford.'

Perhaps he was, thought Agatha with a sudden stab of pity. But whatever Charles had been at one time in his life, it had obviously been something better than sitting under the arches at Waterloo scrambling what was left of his brains.

The night wore on. Fights broke out. Women cried, long maudlin wails for lost men and lost children. It's not a seductive way of life, thought Agatha. It's a foretaste of hell. There was a brief scramble of activity when the Silver Lady came round, a van with sandwiches and hot coffee, some of them trying to trade their sandwiches and coffee for another swig of drink.

Gradually, like animals, they crept off into their packing-cases. Still this Lizzie had not come.

Dawn was rising over grimy London. A blackbird perched up on a rooftop sent down a chorus of glorious sound, highlighting the degradation and misery and wasted lives of those in the packing-cases beneath.

Agatha got stiffly to her feet. 'I've had it, Roy. Give your detective lady the job of finding Lizzie and double her pay to do it. I'm going home.'

'Haven't we even got enough between us for the tube?' asked Roy.

Agatha scraped in her pockets and finally found a pound. 'That's for me to take the tube,' she said firmly.

'You'll have to stick with me, sweetie, if you want to get into the office to get your bag and car keys. I have the keys to the office.'

'Let me have them.'

'No.'

'Do you mean you're going to make me walk back all that way?'

'Yes.'

Not speaking to each other, each stiff and sore and exhausted from their long night and with queasy stomachs from the awful mixture they had drunk, they headed in the direction of Waterloo station.

A well-dressed man in evening dress approached them. He stood in front of them, stopping their progress, his face a mixture of pity and disgust. He fished in his pocket, took out his wallet and extracted a ten-pound note. 'For God's sake,' he said to Roy, 'get your mother a decent breakfast and don't spend this on booze.'

'Oh, thank you, thank you.' Roy seized the note.

'Taxi!' he yelled, and, miracle of miracles, a taxi came to a stop. Roy shoved Agatha inside, shouted, 'Cheapside,' and the cab drove off.

The man in evening dress gazed after them in a fury. That's the last time I waste money on people like that, he thought.

James had suffered a sleepless night as well. At first he had thought Agatha was staying away to get revenge, but then he began to think something might have happened to her. At last he settled down in an armchair in front of the cottage window, jumping to his feet every time he heard the sound of a car, but there was only, first, the milkman, and then Mrs Hardy going off early somewhere.

His eyes grew heavier and heavier. Why hadn't she even phoned?

He fell asleep at last and in his dream he was marrying Helen Warwick. He only knew he did not want to marry Helen but that somehow she had blackmailed him into it. He was standing at the altar, hoping that Agatha Raisin would come and rescue him, when the sound of a key in the lock made his eyes jerk open.

He jumped to his feet, shouting, 'Agatha! Where the hell have you been?'

Agatha had not bothered to change out of her down-and-out outfit. James stared at the wreck that was Agatha, the black circles under her eyes and the terrible smell of stale booze mixing with the meths with which she had sprinkled her clothes at the beginning of the masquerade.

'Oh, Agatha,' he said, looking at her, pity in his eyes replacing the anger. 'I really thought Helen Warwick might have had something else to say, something useful. But if I had known it would upset you so much . . .'

Agatha sat down wearily. 'The vanity of men never ceases to amaze me. I did not go out and get sozzled because my heart was broken, James dear. Roy and I dressed up and went down to the packing-cases of Waterloo, where we spent the night. We found out something useful. Jimmy had a bag of stuff which a woman called Lizzie took away. We're going to get Roy's detective to try to track her down. Now all I want is to sleep. I nearly drove off the road on the way down here. Enjoy your visit to Helen?'

'No,' said James curtly. 'Big mistake. Gold-digger.'

Agatha gave a little smile and headed for the stairs.

'And burn those clothes,' yelled James after her.

Chapter Eight

Suddenly it seemed to Agatha that, after that adventure, everything went quiet. Mrs Hardy begged an extra week. She had found a place in London but needed the extra time until the flat became available. *The Bugle* finally learned about the attempted shooting and ran some of the original interview with Agatha. At first there was hope that someone who knew something about Mrs Gore-Appleton would come forward, but no one appeared to know anything of any importance. In fact, several people had contacted the police, people who had worked for her charity on a voluntary basis. But their descriptions did not add very much to what the police already knew. Bill Wong privately thought that Mrs Gore-Appleton was probably settled comfortably in some foreign country where they could not reach her.

He called round one evening, saying dismally to James and Agatha that he was beginning to fear they would never get her now.

'What's this Fred Griggs was saying about the murder of Miss Purvey not being connected with the case?'

'There have been a couple of random stabbings in that cinema and we got some nutter for them. He says he strangled the Purvey woman.'

'And you believe him?'

'I don't, but everyone else seems determined to have one of the murders solved. Have you two found out anything?'

James looked at Agatha and Agatha looked at James. Agatha was still smarting over the Maddie episode. She did not know Maddie was off the case. If she told Bill about Roy's detective looking for the mysterious Lizzie, then the police would take over, Maddie might get some of the credit, and Agatha felt she could not bear that.

'No, nothing,' she said. 'I'm moving back next door.'

'When?'

'Just over two weeks now. It would have been sooner, but Mrs Hardy begged the extra time. She's found a place in London.'

'Did that article in the newspaper not prompt anyone to come forward with information about Mrs Gore-Appleton?' asked James.

'Yes, it did. Mostly rich, retired ladies who did voluntary work for her. Some had contributed quite a lot of money to the charity, but others hung on to their wallets when they realized that Mrs Gore-Appleton only made a few token visits down among London's homeless, dispensing clothes and food. The description is pretty much what we had before – hard, middle-aged, muscular, blonde.'

'Didn't she have any friends among them?'

'No, they only saw her during office hours. They all remember Jimmy Raisin. Mrs Gore-Appleton was very proud of him, they said. She said it all showed what a little kindness and care could do. Two of the ladies got the impression that Mrs Gore-Appleton and Jimmy were lovers.'

'Well, we can't blame Jimmy for corrupting her, as she was running a bent charity when they met. How did she get away with it? She would need to be registered with the Charities Commission.'

'She never did that. Just hung out her shingle, didn't advertise for volunteers, simply canvassed a few churches. Quite a scam, in a way. One woman gave her fifteen thousand pounds, and she was the only one who would admit to the amount she paid, so goodness knows what she got from the others.'

Agatha thought of the waste of humanity she had spent the night with under the arches, all God's lost children, and felt a surge of fury. Mrs Gore-Appleton had, in her own sweet way, been robbing the poor.

'I can't bear the idea that she should get away with it. At the moment, the villagers have dropped the idea that either James or myself did it, but I met the horrible Mrs Boggle in the village shop the other day, and she sneered at me darkly about "some folks can get away with murder". If the case isn't solved, then who knows? Everyone might start to think that way again.'

'I'll let you know anything I can,' said Bill.

'How are things?' asked Agatha. 'I mean with you.'

'Maddie? Oh, that's finished. My mother is quite pleased, and so is Dad. I thought they would be disappointed, because they both hope to see me married.'

Agatha privately thought Mr and Mrs Wong would do anything in their power to drive off any female interested in their precious son, but did not say so, which went to show she had changed slightly for the better. The old Agatha had been totally blind and deaf to anyone else's feelings.

But she saw the pain at the back of Bill's eyes and felt a surge of hatred for Maddie.

'So what happens now with you two?' asked Bill.

There was an awkward silence and then Agatha said brightly, 'We'll soon be back to normal – me in my small cottage and James in his. We can wave to each other over the fence.'

'Oh, well, I'm sure you'll sort something out,' said Bill. 'I'm glad to see you've given up investigating murders, Agatha. Not that you weren't a help in the past, but mostly because of your blundering about and making things happen.'

Agatha looked at him, outraged. 'You can go off people, you know.'

'Sorry. Just my joke. But you've nearly got yourself killed in the past. Don't do it again.' His face beamed. 'I'd hate to lose you.'

Agatha smiled suddenly. 'There are times when I wish you were much older, Bill.'

He smiled back. 'And there are times I wish I were, Agatha.'

'Do you want coffee, Bill?' asked James sharply.

'What? Oh, no, I've got to be going.'

Agatha followed him to the door. 'Don't stay away too long. When I'm back in my own place, come for dinner.'

'That's a date. And nothing microwaved either.'

He kissed her on the cheek and went off whistling.

'Oh, God,' said Agatha, coming back into the living-room, where James was moodily kicking at the rug in front of the fireplace. 'I've just remembered. We're hosting the Ladies' Society from Ancombe. I'd better get along to the village hall. I know what. I'll see if Mrs Hardy wants to come.'

'Do what you want,' muttered James.

Agatha stared at him. 'What's got into you?'

'I haven't been writing,' he said. He went and sat down in front of the computer and switched it on.

Agatha shrugged and went upstairs. Love sometimes came in waves, like flu, but she was temporarily free of the plague and hoped to make it permanent.

She came back downstairs whistling the same tune she had heard Bill whistling when he left. James was glowering at the screen of the computer.

'I'm off,' said Agatha brightly.

No reply.

'It was nice of Bill to call.' She gave a little laugh. 'I sometimes wonder why he bothers with me.'

'He comes,' said James acidly, 'to get a tan from the light that shines from the hole in your arse.'

Agatha stared at James, her mouth dropping. James turned bright red.

'You're jealous,' said Agatha slowly.

'Don't be ridiculous. The thought of you and a man as young as Bill Wong is disgusting.'

'But definitely intriguing,' said Agatha. 'See you later.'

She went out feeling an unaccustomed little surge of power.

Mrs Hardy was at home, and after a certain show of reluctance said she would accompany Agatha to the village hall.

'What's in store?' asked Mrs Hardy.

'I don't really know,' said Agatha. 'I'm usually very much part of the arrangements, but with all the frights and running around, I've had nothing to do with this one. But whatever it is, you'll enjoy it.'

Agatha's heart sank when they entered the hall and she learned from Mrs Bloxby that the Carsely Ladies' Society were giving a concert.

'How can we do that?' hissed Agatha. 'I didn't think we had anyone who could perform anything.'

'I think you'll be surprised,' said Mrs Bloxby blandly and moved away to help the grumbling Mrs Boggle out of her wraps.

Mrs Hardy and Agatha were handed printed programmes.

The first performer was to be Miss Simms, the society's secretary, who was billed to sing 'You'll Never Walk Alone'.

But the opening number was a line-up of the village ladies performing a Charleston, dressed in twenties outfits. Agatha blinked. Where on earth had the portly Mrs Mason come by that beaded dress? Mrs Mason, she remembered, had threatened to leave the village after her niece had been found guilty of murder, but she had finally elected to stay and no one ever mentioned the murder. The ladies did quite well, apart from occasionally bumping into one another on the small stage.

Then Miss Simms walked forward and adjusted the microphone. She was still wearing the skimpy flapper dress she had worn for the opening number. She opened her mouth. Her voice was thin and reedy, screeching on the high notes and disappearing altogether in the low notes. Agatha had never realized before what a very long song it was. At last it was mercifully over. Fred Griggs then took up a position on the stage in front of a table full of rings and scarves. Fred fancied himself as a conjurer. He got so many things wrong that the kindly village audience decided he was doing it deliberately and laughed their appreciation. The only person not joining in the laughter was Fred, who grew more and more anguished. At last a large box like a wardrobe was wheeled on the stage, and Fred nervously asked for a volunteer for the vanishing-lady trick.

Mrs Hardy walked straight up the aisle and climbed on the stage.

Fred whispered to her and she went into the box and he shut the door.

'Ladies and gentlemen,' said Fred. 'I will now make this lady vanish.'

He waved his stick and two schoolchildren turned the box round and round.

Then Fred, with a flourish, opened the door. Mrs Hardy had vanished.

Warm applause.

Fred beamed with relief and signalled to the schoolchildren, who revolved the box again.

'Viola!' cried Fred. He meant '*Voilà*,' thinking French some magical language. He opened the door. His face fell and he slammed it shut again and muttered something to the schoolchildren. The box was revolved again.

Again Fred cried, 'Viola!' and opened the door.

No Mrs Hardy.

It must be part of the act, thought the audience, as Fred, with his face red and sweating, began to search inside the box.

'You couldn't even find my cat,' shouted Mrs Boggle. 'No wonder you can't find that woman. Can't even find your brains on a good day, Fred.'

Fred glared down at her. Then he bowed. Schoolchildren ran forward to clear his props from the stage and a villager called Albert Grange came on and began to play the spoons.

Agatha slipped out of her seat and went quickly out of the village hall. She hurried towards Lilac Lane. She was beginning to wonder if something awful had happened to Mrs Hardy.

And then, as she turned the corner into Lilac Lane, she saw the stocky figure of Mrs Hardy in front of her.

'Mrs Hardy!' called Agatha.

She swung round.

'Whatever happened?' asked Agatha, coming up to her.

'It was such a boring, awful affair,' said Mrs Hardy with a grin, 'that I just walked out of the back of the box and out of the back of the hall.'

'But poor Fred,' protested Agatha.

'Why bother? He'd got everything else so mucked up that I reckoned another failure wouldn't matter.'

Agatha looked at her doubtfully. 'It seems a bit cruel to me.'

'I can't make you out,' said Mrs Hardy. 'I know you used to run a successful business and yet here you rot, wasting your time and energy going to a dreadful affair like that. How can you bear it? I've never met such a dreary bunch of yokels in my life before.'

'They're not dreary! They are very kind and warmhearted.'

'What? People like that smelly old Boggle woman? Those pathetic village women cavorting around in the Charleston? Get a life!'

Agatha's eyes narrowed. 'I was beginning to think

206

you were all right. But you're not. I'm glad you're leaving Carsely. You don't belong here.'

'No one whose brains haven't turned into mush belongs here.'

'There are brilliant people living in the Cotswolds! Writers.'

'Middle-aged menopausal women churning out Aga sagas about naughty doings in the vicarage? Ancient, creaking geriatrics making arrangements out of dried flowers and painting bad watercolours and all pretending to be upper-class?'

'Mrs Bloxby is a good example of all that is fine about village life.'

'The vicar's wife? A sad creature who lives through other people because she has no life of her own. Oh, don't let's quarrel. You like it. I don't. I'll see you later.'

Agatha went slowly back to the village hall. A woman she only knew slightly was at the microphone singing 'Feelings'. Mr and Mrs Boggle had fallen asleep.

Agatha sat down and looked about her. Mrs Hardy's words seeped like poison into her brain. How pathetic and shabby the village hall looked. Rain had begun to fall, blurring the high windows. Surely there *was* more to life than this. Perhaps her loneliness had caused her to look at the whole thing through a pair of distorting, rose-tinted glasses. And what of her non-relationship with James? A woman of any maturity, of any guts and courage would have given him up as a bad job. And what would married life with him have been like anyway? He was handsome and clever, but so self-contained, so *cold*, that even if they were married, life would be pretty much the same. And what about sex? Didn't he miss it? Didn't he ever think of the nights they had spent together?

It seemed to Agatha that he preferred to return to a life of celibacy, a celibacy broken by a few affairs.

She had never really given London a chance. Yes, she had been friendless there, but that was because of the way she had gone on. She had changed. She had invested the money from the sale of her business very well. She would not need to work if she returned to London.

The concert mercifully drew to a close with the cast singing 'That's Entertainment'.

Then there was a general movement as chairs were drawn back and tables were set out for the lunch in honour of the Ancombe ladies. Agatha shivered. The hall was cold. Lunch turned out to be the inevitable quiche and salad. There was not even any home-made wine to wash it down, as there usually was at these functions, only rather dusty tea.

Conversation was desultory. Agatha looked around. What have I done? she wondered. How could I ever have thought I would fit in here? I don't really belong. I wasn't born in a village, I was born in a Birmingham slum, where trees and flowers were things you ripped out of the earth as soon as they dared to show a leaf. There was a lot to be said after all for anonymous

London. Perhaps Bill Wong would come up and visit her from time to time. Well, maybe Mrs Bloxby, too. As for James . . . well, she, Agatha Raisin, was worth better than James Lacey. She wanted a man with red blood in his veins, a man capable of intimacy, warmth, affection.

'Dark thoughts?'

The woman who had been sitting at one of the long tables next to Agatha had left. Mrs Bloxby had slid into her place.

'I don't really belong here,' said Agatha, waving a hand about the room. 'And do you know, I'm worth better than James. I want someone capable of intimacy. I don't mean sex. I mean warmth and affection.'

Mrs Bloxby looked at her doubtfully. 'I have thought that perhaps the attraction James Lacey holds for you is because he lacks those things. By the very absence of them, the relationship lacks proper commitment. It did cross my mind recently that you were more like two bachelors living together than man and woman. And I wonder how you would cope with a man who demanded intimacy and love and affection from you, Mrs Raisin.'

'Agatha.'

'Yes of course, Agatha.'

'I should think myself in seventh heaven.'

'Why this sudden disgust at Carsely and all who sail in her?'

Agatha bit her lip. She was too proud to admit she had been influenced by Mrs Hardy.

'I just thought of it,' she said.

The vicar's wife studied her averted face for a moment and then said, 'I saw you leave the hall shortly after Mrs Hardy disappeared. Did you find her?'

'Yes, she was heading home.'

'Did she give any reason for humiliating Fred Griggs in that way?'

Agatha still did not want to repeat any of Mrs Hardy's remarks about the village and villagers.

'I think Mrs Hardy considered Fred had already humiliated himself and wanted to leave and saw a convenient way to do it.'

'Ah,' said Mrs Bloxby, 'perhaps my first impression of her was right.'

'That being?'

'That she was an unkind and unhappy woman.'

'Oh, no, I think she's a bit like me, used to a faster pace of life.'

'Is that what she tried to make you think?'

'I am not influenced by what anyone says to me,' said Agatha defiantly.

'And yet you have appeared quite contented with all us rustics up till now.'

'Perhaps it's the cold in this hall and the weather, and that was a truly dreadful concert,' said Agatha.

'Yes, it was awful, wasn't it? But then the Ancombe ladies' concert was pretty dire as well.'

'Why do they do it to each other?'

'Everyone likes their moment on stage. There's a bit of the failed actor in all of us. At these village affairs, everyone gets a chance to perform, no matter how bad they are. People applaud and are kind, because all of them want their time in the limelight as well.'

The old steam radiators against the wall gave a preliminary rattle.

'There you are,' said Mrs Bloxby, 'the heating has come on. And look, the Ancombe ladies have brought a case of apple brandy, so we can all have a drink during the speeches. The atmosphere will soon lighten.'

The combination of heat and apple brandy did appear to work wonders. Agatha began to relax. Instead of standing outside looking in, she began to feel part of it again. The chairwoman of the Ancombe Ladies' Society made a speech and told several jokes which were received with gales of laughter.

Stuff London and Mrs Hardy, thought Agatha. I'm happy here.

Agatha and James went out for dinner that evening. James appeared to have recovered his good humour and he wanted to discuss 'our murder case'. Agatha was too content at having regained her feeling of being at home in the country to crave a more personal conversation, but James did start by asking her to remember all she could about her late husband. 'How did you meet him, for example?'

Agatha had quite forgotten that, through snobbery, she had hidden her low beginnings from James, always implying without actually saying so that she had come from a middle-class background and had been to a private school.

'How did I meet Jimmy?' Agatha sighed and put down her knife and fork and looked back down the long years.

'Let me see. I'd just escaped from home.'

'Home being Birmingham?'

'Yes, one of those blocks of flats in what they now call the inner city but what they used to call a slum.' She was so intent on her memories that she did not notice the flicker of surprise in James's blue eyes.

'Ma and Dad always seemed to be drunk. They wouldn't let me stay at school after I was fifteen, even though the teachers begged them to let me complete my education. They put me to work in a biscuit factory. God, the women seemed coarse, brutal. I was a skinny, sensitive little wimp then.

'I saved as much as I could and took off for London one night when my parents were both drunk. I was determined to be a secretary. The secretaries I had seen up in the offices of the biscuit factory looked fabulous creatures to me, compared to what I was working with on the shop floor. So I got a job as a waitress and went to a secretarial college in the evenings to learn shorthand and typing. I worked seven days a week, and my ambition was so great, I don't think my feet ached once. It

212

wasn't a very classy restaurant. Classy restaurants only employed waiters in those days. It was a bit like one of the Lyon's Corner Houses. Good food but not French, if you know what I mean.'

Her eyes grew dreamy. 'Jimmy came in one night. He was with a rather tarty blonde, a bit older than he was. They seemed to be quarrelling. Then he started to flirt with me and that made her even angrier. I didn't think he was interested in me. I thought he was only doing it to get back at his girlfriend for something or other.

'But when I left by the back door that night after work, he was waiting for me. He said he would see me home. I had been working the evening shifts as well as the day ones while the secretarial college was closed for the summer vacation. He was very . . . merry. Very light-hearted. I'd never met anyone quite like Jimmy before.

'We got to my place, which was a bed-sit in Kilburn. I asked him where he lived and he said he had nowhere, because he had just been thrown out of his digs. I asked him where his stuff was and he said it was in the left luggage in Victoria station. All he had in the world was one suitcase.

'I said he could sleep on the sofa just for one night. He did that. But the next day was a rare day off and we went to the zoo. Funny. I never liked zoos and I still don't, but I had been so very lonely and here I was with a handsome fellow of my own and it all seemed marvellous. Somehow it was agreed, I don't remember how, that he would move in with me. Of course he wanted to

213

sleep with me, but the pill hadn't really got going in those days, and I was terrified of getting pregnant. He just laughed and said we'd get married. And so we did. We went to Blackpool on our honeymoon.'

Agatha suddenly looked at James and realized that she had finally betrayed all the truth of her background. Then she gave a little shrug and went on.

'He got a job loading newspapers down in Fleet Street. I was still working as a waitress and going to the college. It took me a month of marriage to realize I had jumped right out of the frying-pan into the fire, that is, I had jumped from a drunken home life into marriage to a drunken husband.

'To this day, I don't know why he ever married me. I mean, he was very attractive to women. He began to hit me. I hit back because I was still thin but pretty wiry. And then, I wasn't drunk, and he was.

'He lost his job and drifted from one to another after that, but mostly was out of work. I stuck at it for two years. But I'd landed a job in a public relations firm as a secretary and I wanted money for good clothes and I wouldn't keep him in drink any more. I came back one evening and he was lying on the bed, snoring, with his mouth open. On the mat the post was lying unopened and in the post was a package of literature from Alcoholics Anonymous that I'd sent for. I pinned it on his chest, packed my things and left.

'He knew where I worked and I fully expected him to come after me, looking for money. But he never came.

214

Gradually the years went by and I was really sure he was dead. I thought no one could drink that much and go on living. Ambition took over completely. So what did I know of Jimmy? He had great charm. Hard for you to believe now. When I first met him, he had a way of making me feel like the only woman in the world that mattered, and he was the only man in my life who ever made me feel pretty. He never said anything clever and his jokes were always feeble, but before it all went sour, he made me feel good, made me feel exhilarated, as if the world was a funny place where nothing much mattered.' Agatha heaved a little sigh. 'Will the real Jimmy Raisin stand up? I don't know. At first, after each drinking bout he would be genuinely contrite. Oh, I know. He always talked about making money and he was always sure he would make it. I suppose he lived on dreams.'

'And I gather,' said James harshly, 'that he was a budding con artist when you met him. Too lazy to work. He got a taste through you of the benefits of being kept by a woman. You had got wise to him. So he probably sobered up just long enough to get some other female involved. What you have described, Agatha, is a greedy, selfish man. A natural blackmailer.'

'I suppose I've told you nothing you didn't know already,' said Agatha in a small voice.

'Not really. Except I did not know that you had such a hard life.'

'Did I? Ambition is a great drug, you know. I just forged ahead the whole time. Never really looked back

215

at yesterday. Anyway, to get back to this murder, or murders. It must be one of the people that Jimmy met at the health farm. I've come back to that idea. I wish that Comfort woman hadn't escaped us. I think she was lying to us.'

'There was certainly something about our visit that sent her running off to Spain,' said James. 'Then there's her ex. He was very truculent.'

'But he wasn't even at the health farm,' protested Agatha. 'How would he know what Jimmy and Miss Purvey looked like?'

'It could be the something that Gloria was lying about. Perhaps Jimmy didn't write to Mr Comfort. Perhaps he called on him.'

'Fine. So what about Miss Purvey?'

'If Miss Purvey's murder was not connected to Jimmy's, it might make the field wider.'

'I think our only hope is that Roy's detective might find something in that bag that the mysterious Lizzie took.'

Agatha sneezed.

'Are you getting a cold?' asked James.

'I don't know. I might have a bit of a chill. That church hall was freezing today during the concert.'

'Home and bed, then. We'll think some more about it tomorrow.'

As they were driving down into Carsely, a car passed them going the other way. James braked suddenly. 'I think that was Helen Warwick! She must have been to see us.'

'To see you, you mean,' said Agatha.

'I'd better catch up with her.' James swung the wheel around.

'What for?' demanded Agatha as they began to race back up the way Helen Warwick had taken. 'You said she had nothing more to tell us.'

'But she must have had, for why did she come all this way to see us?'

'To murder us in our beds,' said Agatha gloomily.

All the way down the hill and towards Moreton-in-Marsh, James looked ahead for Helen's car. She had been driving a BMW. He saw one ahead at the first round-about in Moreton. They managed to catch up with it on the Oxford road, only to find that the driver was an elderly man, not Helen Warwick.

They drove on a few more miles before James said reluctantly, 'That's that. We've missed her.'

'I'm not sorry,' said Agatha. 'She only came down here to chase after you.'

'Probably right,' agreed James, and Agatha scowled at him in the darkness. By the time they got home, she was coughing and wheezing and her head felt as if it were on fire.

At James's urging, she took two aspirins and went to bed and plunged down into a hell of noisy dreams, of raging fires, of gunshots, and of running and running along the Embankment in London with Roy at her heels, both of them fleeing from someone they did not know.

The next day Agatha felt too ill to care about anything at all. She lay in bed all day, drifting in and out of sleep. James carried in snacks on trays and bottles of mineral water for her. Agatha refused to let him call the doctor, saying that all she had was a bad cold, and if there were a cure for the common cold, it would have been front-page headlines by now.

At seven in the evening, she heard the doorbell and then the sound of voices and James's voice raised in sudden shock. 'What!'

She groaned and fumbled for her dressing-gown. Cold or no cold, red nose or no red nose, she simply had to find out what was going on.

She made her way down the stairs and into the living-room. At first she thought the scene before her eyes was part of a fever-induced hallucination. There was Wilkes, flanked by Bill Wong and two constables.

She blinked and realized they really were there and said, 'Why are they here, James?'

James's face was set and grim.

'Helen Warwick has been murdered.'

Agatha sat down suddenly.

'Oh, no. When?'

'Today. Strangled with one of her scarves. And she

218

tried to see us last night, Agatha. She was here, in Carsely, last night, and now she's dead.'

Wilkes said, 'Unfortunately no one at the flats where she lives saw anything. We guess the murder took place somewhere in the middle of the afternoon. We are taking statements from everyone who knew her.'

'As you can see,' said James, pointing at Agatha, 'Mrs Raisin was in no fit state to go anywhere, and I was acting nursemaid. I was down at the local store twice to get groceries. They will vouch for me.'

'You went to see her,' said Bill Wong suddenly. It was a statement, not a question. 'Couldn't you have left it to us?'

James said wearily, 'I honestly don't see that our visit was any different to a visit from you, say.'

They took James over and over again what Helen had said, and then why he had gone back. Agatha coughed and shivered. She was beginning to feel too ill to care.

At last the police left.

'Back to bed, Agatha,' said James. 'There's nothing we can do tonight.'

But Agatha tossed and turned for a long time. Somewhere out there was a murderer, a murderer who, having tried to burn them to death, might try again.

James was just about to go upstairs to bed himself when the phone rang.

Roy Silver was on the other end of the line, his voice sharp and excited. 'Agatha there?'

'Agatha's very ill with a bad cold. Can I help?'

'It's that woman, Lizzie. Iris has found her. She's got Jimmy's things.'

'Good. And what's in them?'

'I don't know. The old bat is asking for a hundred pounds.'

'Well, pay her, dammit.'

'I don't have any spare cash, James.'

'What's the arrangement for paying her?'

'She'll be at Temple tube station tomorrow at noon.'

'I'll be there, with the money.'

'Iris'll be there as well, with me. She'll point the old bat out to us. Sure I can't speak to Aggie?'

'No, she's too ill. See you tomorrow.'

James replaced the receiver and went upstairs.

'Who was that?' called Agatha.

James knew that if he told Agatha the truth, she would insist on coming. 'Just some reporter from the *Daily Mail*,' he said soothingly. 'Try to sleep.'

The next day, when Agatha finally crept downstairs, it was to find a note from James on the table saying he had gone to police headquarters in Mircester. James did not want there to be any danger of Agatha following him to London.

Agatha trailed into the kitchen and made herself a cup of coffee. The cottage seemed quiet and sinister without James, and it still smelt of burnt wood and paint from the fire. The temporary chipboard door erected by the

220

carpenter to make do until James's insurance claim went through seemed a flimsy barrier against the outside world.

She let her cats out into the garden after feeding them. Her legs felt like jelly. She had another cup of coffee and two cigarettes, each of which tasted vile, and then crawled back to bed.

James approached Temple tube station with a feeling of excitement. If only there would be something, somewhere in Jimmy's things that might give him a clue. He was worried about leaving Agatha alone. It was ten minutes to twelve when he arrived at the tube station. On impulse, he phoned Mrs Hardy and asked her if she would phone Agatha or pop round and see if she was all right. Mrs Hardy answered cheerfully that she wasn't doing anything else and would be happy to look after Agatha, and, reassured, James put the phone down.

He turned round to see Roy and his formidable detective waiting for him. Roy made the introductions.

'Now where is this woman?' asked James, looking around. 'What if she doesn't show?'

'She'll show,' said Iris. 'Just think of all the booze one hundred pounds will buy her.'

'Aggie should be here,' said Roy. 'How is she?'

'Pretty poorly,' said James. 'Look, I didn't tell her about this or she would have come racing up to London and she's not fit.'

'There she is,' said Iris.

A small woman in layers of shabby clothes was shuffling into the tube station. Her eyes were sunk into her head and she had no teeth. She was bent and aged-looking and her hands clutching two plastic bags were twisted and crippled with arthritis.

'Hello, Lizzie,' said Iris briskly. 'Give us the bag.'

'Money first,' said Lizzie. 'I want a thousand pounds.'

Before James or Roy could say anything, Iris said, 'Well, that's that, Lizzie. We'll take our hundred pounds and go. I doubt if there is anything in there worth even a fiver.'

And James saw from the look in Lizzie's eyes that she had already gone through the late Jimmy Raisin's effects and agreed with Iris.

''Ere, wait a minute.' A claw-like hand clutched at Iris's sleeve. 'You got the money?'

Iris nodded to James, who took out his wallet and extracted five twenty-pound notes. Lizzie's eyes gleamed.

'Bag, Lizzie,' prompted Iris.

'The money,' said Lizzie.

'Oh, no. Is this the right bag?' Iris took it from her. 'I'll just have a quick look in here first. It could be nothing but old newspapers.'

Iris looked inside and fumbled around. All Jimmy's worldly goods seemed to consist of a few photographs, a corkscrew, some letters and a battered wallet.

'All right,' said Iris.

James handed over the money. 'I hope you are going to buy yourself some food with this.'

Lizzie looked at him as if he were mad, seized the money and stowed it somewhere under her layers of clothes, and then shambled off.

'Let's go somewhere and look at what we've got,' said James.

'We'll go to my office,' said Iris. 'But you're going to be disappointed. Seems to be nothing but scraps of paper and a few photographs.'

They took a taxi to Iris's office in Paddington and, once there, tipped the contents out on the desk.

There were love letters from various women, damp and crumpled and stained. Jimmy had probably kept them to gloat over. There was a photograph of a thin girl with small eyes and heavy dark brown hair. That was in the wallet and was the only thing it contained. James said, 'By God, it's our Agatha as a girl. You can hardly recognize her.' There were various other photographs of women, and then one of Jimmy on a beach. A middle-aged blonde woman in a swimsuit was rubbing oil on his back. She was thin and muscular. Her face was turned away from the camera. 'Damn, I wish we could see her face,' muttered James. 'I bet that's Mrs Gore-Appleton.'

'Let me see those other photos again.' Iris bent her head and went through them. 'There,' she said triumphantly. 'That's the same woman.'

James found himself looking at a blonde with a thin, aggressive face.

And then, as he stared down at that face, he found himself becoming sure he had seen it before. Agatha had changed amazingly from the days of her youth. People changed. Women changed in middle age, often put on weight.

And suddenly he knew who it was. Let the blonde hair grow out and put on a few stone and you had Mrs Hardy. Yes, the mouth was the same, and the same hard eyes.

'Oh, my God,' he said, 'and I've told her to look after Agatha.'

'Who?' screeched Roy.

'Mrs Hardy. That's Mrs Hardy, our next-door neighbour.'

'I told Agatha it was probably her all along,' said Roy.

James phoned home. No reply. Then he phoned Mrs Hardy. The engaged signal. Beginning to sweat, he phoned Bill Wong and talked urgently.

Chapter Nine

Agatha finally decided that if she had a bath and dressed, she might feel better. She soaked for a long time in the bath and then, returning to her room, dressed in a warm sweater and slacks, looking forward to the day when she could return to her cottage and blast the central heating as much as she wanted. James had his central heating system on a timer so that the radiators pushed out two hours' heat in the morning and two in the evening, which Agatha thought mean.

The phone rang. It was Mrs Hardy. James had said Agatha was ill. Did she want food made or anything?

Agatha was suddenly anxious to get out of the house, even for a short while. 'I'd like a cup of coffee,' she said. 'Be along in a minute.'

She let the cats in from the garden, fed them and, putting her cigarettes in her handbag, went out and headed for next door.

It was only when she was inside and ensconced in the kitchen that Agatha regretted having come. All Mrs Hardy's remarks about the village and the villagers came back into her mind. Also, Agatha began to suspect that Mrs Hardy found her not only an object of pity but slightly amusing. There was a mocking glint in Mrs Hardy's eye when she looked at Agatha, although her voice was kind as she gave her a cup of coffee and said, 'Here. That's some of the good Brazilian stuff from Drury's. You look truly awful. Are you sure you should be out of bed?'

'Yes, I actually feel better than I look,' said Agatha. She cast a proprietorial look about the kitchen. Soon the whole cottage would be hers again.

'What's Mr Lacey doing in London?' asked Mrs Hardy.

'Oh, he's not in London. He's at police headquarters in Mircester. He left me a note.'

'That's odd. He phoned me and told me to look after you. I did the 1471 dialling thing as soon as he had hung up. It was a London number.'

'Maybe he decided to go on from there,' said Agatha.

The phone in the living-room rang out. 'Excuse me.' Mrs Hardy went to answer it. Agatha heard her say, 'No, I haven't seen her today.' The phone was replaced. It promptly rang again. Agatha realized with surprise that Mrs Hardy must have answered it for in the quiet of the cottage she could hear a little tinny voice yapping from the other end and yet Mrs Hardy said nothing in reply. When Mrs Hardy came into the kitchen, Agatha said, 'There's someone on the line. I can hear the voice from here.'

226

'Oh, it's one of those nuisance calls. Heavy breathing and all.' Mrs Hardy went back and slammed down the receiver and then took the phone off the hook.

'I've just remembered,' said Mrs Hardy. 'I have to go out. But stay there and finish your coffee while I go upstairs and get some things.'

Agatha nodded and sipped her coffee. Finally, feeling bored, she got up and looked in the kitchen cupboards in a nosy sort of way. Then she slid open the drawers. In one were some photographs. She flipped through them idly and then stared in amazement. She was looking down at the face of her husband, sitting next to a hard-faced blonde woman, somewhere in France at an outdoor café.

And then as she looked closer she remembered something about this Mrs Gore-Appleton having taken Jimmy to the south of France. The face looked familiar. Those eyes with the mocking look, that hard mouth.

She slowly closed the drawer and stood hanging on to the kitchen counter. What fools they had all been. It was so dreadfully simple. Mrs Hardy was Mrs Gore-Appleton. It must have been she who recognized Miss Purvey in the cinema that day, even though she had said she was going to London. The mercenary Helen Warwick must somehow have decided to call on James and spotted Mrs Gore-Appleton and recognized her. They must have spoken.

Mrs Gore-Appleton was so changed in appearance that Helen might have said something like, 'Aren't you that woman I met at the health farm?' Something like that. And did Mrs Gore-Appleton try to bribe her? Say she would call on her in London? What was the address? That sort of thing. And Helen might have gone along with it, hoping to make some money.

The sound of Mrs Gore-Appleton coming down the stairs made Agatha's blood freeze.

Had Agatha not been so disoriented by the fever, which was rising again, she would have done the sensible thing and left immediately and called the police. But a sort of dizzy outrage took hold of her and she said, 'Mrs Gore-Appleton, I presume.' She jerked a thumb over her shoulder. 'I saw the photo of you and Jimmy in that drawer.'

'You truly are a village person, poking your nose into things.' Mrs Gore-Appleton was standing there, her bulk blocking the doorway.

Agatha could have asked her why she had murdered three people, but instead she heard herself saying stupidly, 'Why Carsely? And why this cottage?'

'I wanted out of London,' said Mrs Gore-Appleton. 'I'd tried living in Spain, but it didn't suit. I'd asked a house agent to look for a place in the Cotswolds. I was sent several brochures and decided to come down and have a look around. I heard your name mentioned as one of the sellers. I didn't know you had been married to Jimmy, he never mentioned your name or that he had been married, but the name amused me, and so I bought this.'

'And Jimmy came back and recognized you and tried to put the screws on?'

'Exactly. I'd changed my name to Gore-Appleton with some false papers. When I wound up the charity, I just reverted to my old name.'

'Why didn't you kill me?' asked Agatha, her eyes darting this way and that, looking for a weapon.

'Well, do you know, I did try by setting fire to Lacey's cottage but in case some villager saw me at the scene, I had to look as if I was trying to put it out. Then I took rather a liking to you, and I saw a further way to remove any suspicion from myself and so hired someone to play the part of the gunman. That kick of mine was very well rehearsed.'

'Who was that on the phone just now?' demanded Agatha. 'The police?'

'No, it was the interfering vicar's wife, wanting to know where you were for some suspicious reason.'

Agatha braced her shoulders. Mrs Gore-Appleton had no weapon. 'I am going to walk past you and phone the police,' she said.

Mrs Gore-Appleton stood aside. 'I am not going to stop you; I am tired of running. At least they don't have the death penalty any more.'

She stood aside.

Agatha marched past her and into the living-room. She put the receiver back on the hook and lifted it again and began to dial Mircester police headquarters.

Mrs Gore-Appleton, who had crept up behind her, brought a brass poker down hard on Agatha's head.

With a groan, Agatha slumped to the floor.

'Silly woman.' Mrs Gore-Appleton gave her a kick and replaced the receiver.

She went out into the back garden and into the potting-shed at the end and found a spade. She tore out some of Agatha's finest shrubs and tossed them on the lawn and then began to dig a grave, thankful that the soil was loose and easily dug.

Then she returned to the living-room and felt the unconscious Agatha's pulse. She was still alive, but burying would soon solve that problem, thought Mrs Gore-Appleton. She seized Agatha by the ankles and dragged her through the kitchen and out into the garden, Agatha's wounded head leaving a trail of blood across the paving-stones just outside the door. Then across the lawn she was dragged and tipped face-down into the grave.

'RIP, Agatha dear,' she said, and threw the first shovelful of earth into the grave. She was so intent on her job, with her back to the house, that she was not aware of anyone arriving until Fred Griggs seized her and threw her to the ground while Bill Wong jumped into the grave and frantically began shovelling the earth from Agatha with his bare hands.

Agatha regained consciousness in hospital to find Bill Wong sitting beside the bed. 'You're all right,' said Bill. 'But take it easy. I'll get a statement from you later.'

Agatha looked around in a dazed way. She was in a private room. There were flowers everywhere. Then her eyes widened. 'It was Mrs Gore-Appleton all along. What happened?'

'You had a narrow escape,' said Bill. 'She hit you hard with the poker, dug a grave in the garden, and then tried to bury you alive. Are you up to all this? I'll go if you want to.'

'No, stay,' said Agatha weakly, but her eyes began to close and she fell asleep. When she awoke again, she felt much stronger and found out from a doctor that part of her hair had been shaved off and stitches put in her head. After more checks, she was told she would do very well provided she rested quietly. Agatha's next visitor was Mrs Bloxby.

'I am so glad to see you alive,' said the vicar's wife, arranging a bunch of grapes in a bowl. 'Do you know, it was quite a coincidence. I thought and thought what Mrs Hardy – I think I'll call her that because that is her real name – well, I thought what she had said and then I began to think of the fire and the gunman and I began to get a bad feeling. I phoned her to see if you were there, for I had called your cottage first. She said you weren't there and somehow, I cannot explain why, I thought you were. I phoned again and demanded to know if she had seen you and then I realized she had walked away from the phone. Then I thought I heard your voice in the background before the receiver was replaced. I put on my coat and hurried along to Lilac

231

Lane and saw the police car outside. She tried to bury you alive. Such wickedness.'

Bill Wong came in. 'I brought you some chocolate,' he said.

'Sit down,' urged Agatha, 'and tell me all about it.'

'She talked and talked,' said Bill. 'I think she's a bit mad. She had been running her bent charity when she came across Jimmy. He must have been a wreck, but I tell you something. She actually fell in love with him, hence the slim figure and blonde hair and holiday in the south of France. The blackmailing after the health-farm stay was Jimmy's idea, but she went along with it.

'And then, by coincidence, Jimmy saw her the day of your wedding and decided to blackmail her. She gave him her address and told him to call on her early in the morning. She witnessed his row with you, but she was already waiting for him, dressed as a man. We found the size-nine shoes in her wardrobe. She strangled him and thought her worries were over. Then she strangled poor Miss Purvey. She says that Helen Warwick spotted her when she was trying to call on James Lacey. Mrs Gore-Appleton—'

'Easier to call her Mrs Hardy,' prompted Mrs Bloxby.

'Mrs Hardy, then. She had persuaded Helen Warwick that she had nothing to do with the murders, and that if she kept quiet, she would call on her with "a gift". If the silly woman had gone straight to the police, she would be alive today. And you are lucky to be alive, Agatha. She hit you on the back of the head. Did you know who she really was?'

'Yes, I found a photo of her and Jimmy in the kitchen drawer. I had such a cold – that seems to have been beaten out of me – that nothing seemed quite real and like a fool I confronted her and said I was going to phone the police. She seemed so resigned to it all. The one thing that infuriates me is that Roy Silver of all people was sure Mrs Hardy was the culprit. He'll crow over me until the end of time. But what about Mrs Comfort? Why on earth did she suddenly run off to Spain?'

'Plain and simple. She's back and explained she didn't want to be mixed up in a murder inquiry. She was frightened of her ex-husband. Said she dreamed of having him back but then she fell for Basil and found her ex had grown irrationally bad-tempered and violent and was hitting the bottle. Geoffrey has grown eccentric to say the least and the neighbours are complaining about his drunken threats.'

'Silly woman,' said Agatha bitterly. 'What a lot of our time she wasted.' She suddenly looked anxiously at them. 'Where is James? Has he called?'

Bill and Mrs Bloxby exchanged looks.

'Where is he?' demanded Agatha.

'We'd best tell her the truth,' said Mrs Bloxby.

'She didn't murder *him*? Oh, God, is he all right?'

Mrs Bloxby reached out and grasped Agatha's hand. 'He's all right,' said Bill. 'He found out that Mrs Hardy and Mrs Gore-Appleton were one and the same person. That detective of Roy's had found the mysterious Lizzie and James found a photo of Jimmy Raisin and Mrs Hardy in his effects. Then he realized he had told her to look after you and called me.'

'So where is he?'

Mrs Bloxby's grip grew tighter. 'He made his statement,' said Bill. 'He checked with the hospital to find out if you were okay and then he took off for northern Cyprus. He said he felt he just had to get away. The removal firm that Mrs Hardy had ordered up called for her stuff and the police have taken away any evidence they needed. James put your stuff from his cottage into yours. I'm sorry, Agatha. I had a bit of a row with him. I suggested the least he could do was wait until you regained consciousness.'

'Well, that's that,' said Agatha brightly, although her eyes glittered. 'You win some, you lose some. I'm feeling a little tired now, so . . .'

'Of course.' Mrs Bloxby got to her feet.

'I'll be round tomorrow for that statement,' said Bill.

Agatha smiled weakly. 'Don't bring Maddie.'

'Wouldn't dream of it.'

When they had left, Agatha began to cry. How could James have done something so callous and vile? She finally sobbed herself to sleep, and her last conscious, miserable thought was that she was the most unloved woman in the world.

As the days passed, Agatha slowly recovered her strength, health and spirits. Roy Silver called and she sent him off with instructions to phone the storage company, get them to bring all her goods back and put them in her cottage.

Roy was all too eager to help. Had Mr Wilson not promised him a large bonus if he could lure Agatha back into the fold of public relations?

He returned again two days later to tell her brightly that everything was back as it should be and that Doris Simpson, her cleaner, was looking after the cats.

'And I found this on your kitchen table,' said Roy, handing her a letter.

Agatha opened it. It was from James. She put it down. 'I'll read it later.'

'So it's all been quite an adventure,' said Roy, 'although that friend of yours, Bill Wong, got all the credit in the newspapers, not a word about us.'

'You deserved a mention,' said Agatha, 'but no credit to me that the case was solved. What a fool I was! A few more bodies and that wretched woman would have gone down in history as a serial killer.'

Roy sat down on the edge of the bed. 'I tell you, Aggie, this village life is not for you. Much too dark and dangerous.'

Agatha grinned. 'I know what you are up to, Roy, and I know why you are being so helpful. I'm grateful to you for arranging all my bits and pieces, but I do not think I really want to go back to work again.'

'I think you owe me something,' said Roy. 'Who got the detective in the first place?'

'You did. And for a very nasty reason.'

'I did it out of friendship,' said Roy huffily. 'You would have been lying dead in your own garden pushing up the daisies if it hadn't been for little old me. Come on, Aggie. Now that that total shit, Lacey, has cleared off the scene, you'll need something to take your mind off all this. What about just another six months?' Agatha had previously worked for six months at Pedmans.

Agatha frowned. It just might work. Every time she thought about James, she got a dull ache in her stomach. Hearts did not break, but it sometimes felt that guts could be torn apart.

'All right,' she said. 'But only a six-month stretch.'

'Aggie, you're a wonder. I'll just go off and phone Wilson.'

When he had gone, Agatha opened the letter again. 'Dear Agatha,' she read,

I know you are going to think me every kind of a rat, running off to Cyprus like this, but I did stay long enough to see that you were recovering. The fact is, I desperately need some time to myself, and I am afraid

236

if I stay around to see you again, I might not leave, and I really do not honestly think I am ready for marriage yet. Please forgive me. I think I love you as much as it is possible for me to love anyone. Do remember that.

Yours,
James.

Agatha put the letter down and stared into space. Hope flared up again in her damaged soul. She read that one bit over and over again. 'I think I love you as much as it is possible for me to love anyone.'

She rang the bell beside the bed.

'Am I getting out of here tomorrow?'

'Yes, Mrs Raisin,' said the nurse.

'Well, be an angel and get me the necessary signing-off forms because I'm leaving today.'

'If you think that's wise . . .'

'Oh, very, very wise.'

'Very well.'

As she left, Roy Silver came in. 'Wilson's delighted, Agatha. Start in a month's time?'

'Sure, sure,' said Agatha, and he looked at her suspiciously. 'Don't glare at me, Roy. I'm here until tomorrow anyway. Aren't you expected back in London?'

'Yes, but don't run away.'

'I'm here in a hospital bed, aren't I?'

Roy left and walked slowly down the corridor. As he passed a nurse who was talking to a doctor, he heard her say, 'That Mrs Raisin in room five wants to check out today. She's not due to leave until tomorrow. I don't suppose a day matters.'

They walked off. Roy stood stock-still. Then he turned back and stopped again. If Agatha had changed her mind, she might not tell him. He would wait until she left and see that she went straight home.

He waited an hour in the car park until he saw Mrs Bloxby, that vicar's wife, arrive. After another half-hour's wait, Agatha emerged with Mrs Bloxby and got into her car. Roy got into his own car and followed. Instead of going to Carsely, they went straight to Moreton-in-Marsh and stopped outside a travel agent's. Again Roy waited until they emerged. Then he breezed into the travel agent's and said blithely, 'I just saw my friend Mrs Raisin. Off to foreign parts?'

'Yes,' said the travel agent brightly. 'Off to northern Cyprus.'

'When?'

'Tomorrow. Now how can I help you, sir?'

'The old, sly, double-dealing bitch,' screamed Roy, thinking of his lost bonus and lost triumph.

'I beg your pardon, sir?' The travel agent, a smart brunette, looked at him, appalled.

'And stuff you too,' yelled Roy. 'God, I hate women!'

If you enjoyed *The Murderous Marriage*, read on for the
first chapter of the next book in the *Agatha Raisin*
series . . .

Agatha Raisin
and the
Terrible Tourist

Chapter One

Agatha Raisin was a bewildered and unhappy woman. Her marriage to her next-door neighbour, James Lacey, had been stopped by the appearance of a husband she had assumed – hopefully – to be dead. But he was very much alive, that was, until he was murdered. Solving the murder had, thought Agatha, brought herself and James close again, but he had departed for north Cyprus, leaving her alone.

Although life in the Cotswold village of Carsely had softened Agatha around the edges, she was still in part the hard-bitten businesswoman she had been when she had run her own public relations firm in Mayfair before selling up, taking early retirement and moving to the country. And so she had decided to pursue James.

Cyprus, she knew, was partitioned into two parts, with Turkish Cypriots in the north and Greek Cypriots in the south. James had gone to the north and somewhere, somehow, she would find him and make him love her again.

North Cyprus was where they had been supposed to go on their honeymoon and, in her less tender moments, Agatha thought it rather hard-hearted and crass of James Lacey to have gone there on his own.

When Mrs Bloxby, the vicar's wife, called, it was to find Agatha amidst piles of brightly coloured summer clothes.

'Are you taking all those with you?' asked Mrs Bloxby, pushing a strand of grey hair out of her eyes.

'I don't know how long I will be there,' said Agatha. 'I'd better take lots.'

Mrs Bloxby looked at her doubtfully. Then she said, 'Do you think you are doing the right thing? I mean, men do not like to be pursued.'

'How else do you get one?' demanded Agatha angrily. She picked up a swimsuit, one-piece, gold and black, and looked at it critically.

'I have doubts about James Lacey,' said Mrs Bloxby in her gentle voice. 'He always struck me as being a cold, rather self-contained man.'

'You don't know him,' said Agatha defensively, thinking of nights in bed with James, tumultuous nights, but silent nights during which he had not said one word of love. 'Anyway, I need a holiday.'

'Don't be away too long. You'll miss us all.'

'There's not much to miss about Carsely. The Ladies' Society, the church fêtes, yawn.'

'That's a bit cruel, Agatha. I thought you enjoyed them.'

But Agatha felt that a Carsely without James had suddenly become a bleak and empty place, filled from end to end with nervous boredom.

'Where are you flying from?'

'Stansted airport in Essex.'

'How will you get there?'

'I'll drive and leave the car in the long-stay car park.'

'But if you are going to be away for very long, that will cost you a fortune. Let me drive you.'

But Agatha shook her head. She wanted to leave Carsely, sleepy Carsely with its gentle villagers and thatched-roof cottages, behind – and everything to do with it.

The doorbell rang. Agatha opened the door and Detective Sergeant Bill Wong walked in and looked around.

'So you're really going?' he remarked.

'Yes, and don't you try to stop me either, Bill.'

'I don't think Lacey's worth all this effort, Agatha.'

'It's *my* life.'

Bill smiled. He was half Chinese and half English, in his mid-twenties, and Agatha's first friend, for before she moved to the Cotswolds she had lived in a hard-bitten and friendless world.

'Go if you must. Can you bring me back a box of Turkish delight for my mother?'

'Sure,' said Agatha.

'She says you must come over for dinner when you get back.'

Agatha repressed a shudder. Mrs Wong was a dreadful woman and a lousy cook.

She went into the kitchen to make coffee and cut cake and soon they were all sitting around and gossiping about local matters. Agatha felt her resolve begin to weaken. She had a sudden clear picture of James Lacey's face turning hard and cold when he saw her again, but thrust it out of her mind.

She was going and that was that.

Stansted airport was a delight to Agatha after her previous experience of the terrible crowds at Heathrow. She found she could smoke not only in the departure lounge but at the gate itself. There were a few British tourists and expatriates. The expatriates were distinguishable from the tourists because they wore those sort of clothes that the breed always wear – the women in print frocks, the men in lightweight suits or blazers, the inevitable cravats – and all had those strangulated sons- and daughters-of-the-Raj voices. Colonial Britain seemed to be alive and well on Cyprus Turkish Airlines.

As she sat near the gate, she was surrounded mainly by Turkish voices. Her fellow passengers all seemed to have great piles of hand luggage.

The flight departure was announced. Those in the smoking seats were called first. With a happy sigh Agatha made her way on to the plane. She had burnt her boats behind her. There was no turning back now.

The plane soared above the grey, rainy skies and flat fields of Essex and all the passengers applauded wildly. Why were they applauding? wondered Agatha. Do they know something I don't? Is it unusual for one of their planes to take off at all?

The minute the plane wheels were up, the 'No Smoking' sign clicked off and Agatha was soon surrounded by a fog of cigarette smoke. She had a window-seat and next to her was a large Turkish Cypriot woman who smiled at her from time to time. Agatha took out a book and began to read.

Then, just as they were starting to descend to Izmir in western Turkey, where she knew they would have to wait for an hour before taking off again, the plane was hit by the most awful turbulence. The hostesses clung on to the trolleys, which lurched dangerously from side to side. Agatha began to pray under her breath. No one else seemed in the slightest fazed. They fastened their seat-belts and chattered amiably away in Turkish. The expats seemed used to it, and the few tourists like Agatha were frightened to let down the British side by showing fear.

Just when she thought the plane would shake itself apart, the lights of Izmir appeared below and soon they landed. Again, everyone applauded, this time Agatha joining in.

'That was scary,' said Agatha to the woman next to her.

'It was a bit o' fun, love,' said the Turkish Cypriot woman speaking English in the accents of London's

East End. 'I mean, you'd pay for somethin' like that at Disney World.'

After an hour, the plane took off again. Between Turkey and Cyprus they were served with a hard square of bread and goat cheese which looked as if it had been stamped out of a machine, washed down with sour-cherry juice.

Agatha felt the plane beginning to descend again. More turbulence, this time a thunderstorm. The plane lurched and bucked like a wild thing and, looking out of the window, Agatha saw to her dismay that the whole plane appeared to be covered in sheets of blue lightning. Again, the passengers smiled and chatted and smoked.

Agatha could not keep quiet any longer. 'He shouldn't try to land in this weather,' she said to the woman next to her.

'Oh, they can land in anything, luv. Pilot's Turkish. They're good.'

'Ladies and gentles,' said a soothing voice. 'We are shortly about to land at Erçan airport.'

Again noisy applause on landing. Agatha peered out. It had been raining. She shuffled off the back of the plane on to the staircase, which had not been properly attached to the plane and bobbed and dipped and swayed dangerously.

I'll swim home, thought Agatha.

Having successfully reached the tarmac, she realized the heat was suffocating. It was like moving through warm soup. Wearily she walked into the airport buildings. It looked more like a military airport than a civilian one. It had actually been an RAF airfield up until 1975, and not much had been done to it since then.

She waited in a long line at passport control, a great number of the Turkish Cypriots having British passports. Her friend of the aeroplane said behind her, 'Ask them for a form. Don't let them stamp your passport.'

'Why?' asked Agatha, swinging around.

'Because if you want to go to Greece, they won't let you in there if you've got one of our stamps on your passport, but they'll give you a form and stamp that and then you can take it out of your passport, luv, and throw it away afterwards.'

Agatha thanked her, got her form, filled it in and went to wait for her luggage.

And waited.

'What the hell's going on here?' she demanded angrily.

No one replied, although a few smiled at her cheerfully. They talked, they smoked, they hugged each other.

Agatha Raisin, pushy and domineering, had landed among the most laid-back people in the world.

By the time the luggage arrived and she had arranged her two large suitcases on to a trolley and got through customs, she was soaking with sweat and trembling with fatigue.

She had booked into the Dome Hotel in Kyrenia and had told them by telephone before she left England to have a taxi waiting for her.

At first, as she scanned the crowd of waiting faces at the airport, she thought no one was there to meet her. Then she saw a man holding up a card which said, 'Mrs Rashin.'

'Dome Hotel?' asked Agatha without much hope.

'Sure,' said the taxi driver. 'No problem.'

Agatha wondered if there might be some Mrs Rashin looking for a taxi, but she was too tired to care.

She sank thankfully into the back seat. The black night swirled past her beyond the steamy windows. The taxi swung off a dual carriageway, through some army chicanes and then began to climb up a precipitous mountain road. Jagged mountains stood up against the night sky.

Then the driver said, 'Kyrenia,' and far below on her right Agatha could see the twinkling lights of a town – and somewhere down there was James Lacey.

The Dome Hotel is a large building on the waterfront of Kyrenia, Turkish name Girne, which has seen better days and has a certain battered colonial grandeur. There is something endearing about the Dome. Agatha checked in and had her bags carried up to her room. She switched on the air-conditioning, bathed and got ready for bed, too tired to unpack her suitcases.

She stretched out on the bed. But exhausted as she was, sleep would not come. She tossed and turned and then got out of bed again.

She fumbled with the curtains, drew them back, opened the windows and then the shutters.

She walked out on to a small balcony, her anger draining away. The Mediterranean, silvered by moonlight, stretched out before her, calm and peaceful. The air smelt of jasmine and the salt tang of the sea. She leaned her hands on the iron railing at the edge of the balcony and took deep breaths of warm air. The waves of the sea crashed on the rocks below and to her left was a sea-water swimming pool carved out of the rock.

When she returned to her room, she found she was beginning to scratch at painful bites on her neck and arms. Mosquitoes! She found a tube of insect-bite cream in her luggage and applied it generously. Then she lay down on the bed again after having closed the windows and shutters.

She dialled reception.

'*Effendim?*' said a weary voice on the phone.

'There is a mosquito in my room,' snapped Agatha.

'*Effendim?*'

'Oh, never mind,' growled Agatha.

Despite the buzzing of the mosquito and her fear of getting more bites – for if she did meet James and they went swimming she did not want to be covered in unsightly lumps – her eyes began to close.

There was a knock at the door. 'Come in,' she called.

A hotel servant came in carrying a fly-swat. His black eyes ranged brightly around the room. Then he swiped hard with the fly-swat.

'Gone now,' he said cheerfully.

Agatha thanked him and tipped him.

Her eyes closed again and she plunged into a nightmare where she was trying and trying to get to north Cyprus but the plane had been diverted to Hong Kong.

When she awoke in the morning, gladness flooded her. She was here in Cyprus and somewhere out in that jasmine-scented world was James.

She put on a smart flowered cotton dress and sandals and went downstairs for breakfast. The dining-room overlooked the sea.

There were a number of Israeli tourists, which puzzled Agatha, who knew this to be a Muslim country, and did not know that Turkish Muslims have a great admiration for Judaism. There were also mainland Turkish tourists – that too, she found out later, when she began to be able to tell the difference between Turk and Turkish Cypriot. But the British tourists were immediately recognizable by their clothes, their white sheepish faces, that odd irresolute look of the British abroad.

The air-conditioning was working in the restaurant. Agatha helped herself from an odd buffet selection which included black olives and goat cheese, and then, anxious to begin the hunt, walked out of the hotel.

She let out a whimper as the full force of the heat struck her. British to the core, Agatha just had to complain to someone. She marched back in and up to the reception desk.

250

'Is it always as hot as this?' she snarled. 'I mean, it's September. Summer's over.'

'It's the hottest September for fifty years,' said the receptionist.

'I can't move in this heat.'

He gave an indifferent shrug. Agatha was to find that the receptionist was Turkish and that Turkish hotel servants have had a servility bypass.

'Why don't you go for a sail?' he said. 'You'll get one of the boats round at the harbour. Cooler on the water.'

'I don't want to waste time,' said Agatha. 'I'm looking for someone. A Mr James Lacey. Is he staying here?'

The receptionist checked the records.

'No.'

'Then can you give me a list of hotels in north Cyprus?'

'No.'

'Why not?'

'We haven't got one.'

'Oh, for heaven's sake! Can I hire a car?'

'Next door to the hotel. Atlantic Cars.'

Grumbling under her breath, Agatha went out and into a small car-hire office next door to the hotel. Yes, she was told, she could hire a car and pay with a British bank cheque if she wanted. 'We drive on the British side of the road,' said the car-hire man in perfect English.

Agatha signed the forms, paid for the car hire, and soon she was behind the wheel of a Renault and edging through the crowded streets of Kyrenia. The other

251

drivers were slow but erratic. No one seemed to bother signalling to the right or the left. She pulled into a parking place on the main street, remembering she had a guide to north Cyprus in her handbag, which she had bought in Dillon's bookshop in Oxford before she left. It would surely have a list of hotels. The guidebook, *Northern Cyprus* by John and Margaret Goulding, she noticed for the first time, was actually published by The Windrush Press, Moreton-in-Marsh in the Cotswolds. That seemed to her like a lucky sign. Sure enough, the hotels in Kyrenia were listed. She returned to her room at the Dome and called one after the other, but none had heard of James Lacey.

She settled down in the air-conditioning to read about Kyrenia instead. Although it was called Girne by the Turks, most still used its old name. In the same way Nicosia had become Lefkoşa, but was often still called Nicosia. Kyrenia, she read, is a small northern port and tourist centre with a famously pretty harbour dominated by a castle; founded (as Kyrenia) in the tenth century BC by Achaeans and renamed Corineum by the Romans. It was later walled against pirates and became a centre for the carob trade but fell largely into ruin in 1631 and by 1814 had become home to only a dozen families. It was revived under the British, who improved the harbour and built the road to Nicosia. Prior to the partition of the island after 1974, when the Turks landed to save their own people from being killed by the Greeks, Kyrenia was a popular retirement town for British expatriates.

After 1974 it was settled by refugees from Limassol in the south of the island and once again resumed its role as a genteel resort, with a new harbour to the east of the town.

Agatha put down the guidebook. The mention of the new harbour had reminded her of the receptionist's suggestion of a sail.

She went out again and walked dizzily in the blinding heat round to the harbour, wandering among the basket chairs of the fish restaurants until she saw a board advertising a cruise. It was a yacht called the *Mary Jane*. The skipper saw her studying the board and came along the gangplank and hailed her. He said the cruise cost twenty pounds and included a buffet lunch. They sailed in half an hour and she would have time to go back to the hotel and fetch her swimsuit.

Agatha bought a ticket and said she would be back. She was now too hot to even think of James. The idea of sailing in a sea breeze was too tempting. Let James wait.

Somehow, perhaps because the heat was affecting her brain, she had imagined she would be the only passenger. But there were eight others, and all English.

There were three upper-class ones sporting expensive clothes and loud braying voices, two men and a woman. One man was elderly with a yellowish-white moustache, glasses and a pink scalp where the sun had scorched his bald spot. The other man was tall and thin and sallow and appeared to be married to the woman, who was also tall and thin and sallow but with a deep bosom and a hard air of sexiness about her. They belonged to that stratum which has adopted the very worst manners of the aristocracy and none of the better ones. They shouted at each other rather than spoke and they stared at the other passengers with a sort of 'my God' look in their eyes. Their contemptuous gaze focused in particular on a woman named Rose, middle-aged, blonde-haired with black roots, diamond rings on her long, tapering fingers, who was also accompanied by two men, one quite elderly and the other middle-aged. The three were in their way a sort of mirror image of the upper-class ones, Rose having a sexy appeal, the middle-aged man appearing to be her husband, and the elderly one a friend.

Agatha wished she had brought a book or newspaper to barricade herself behind. The skipper made the introductions. The upper-class ones were Olivia Debenham and her husband George and their friend, Harry Tembleton; the lower-class were the aforementioned Rose, surname Wilcox, her husband Trevor and their friend Angus King. Trevor had a beer belly and a truculent look, cropped fair hair and thick lips. Angus was an old Scotsman with sagging breasts revealed by his open-necked shirt. Like Rose and Trevor, he appeared to be pretty rich. In fact, thought Agatha, they probably belonged to the new rich class of Essex man and woman, risen to prosperity during the Thatcher years, and they could probably buy and sell the upper-class ones who were gazing at them with such contempt. Then there was a dreary couple who said in whispers that they were Alice and Bert Turpham-Jones, and Olivia sniggered and said in a loud aside that having a double-barrelled name these days was no longer what it had been.

Agatha would have been accepted by Olivia, George and Harry, who were monopolizing the small bar, but she had taken a dislike to them and so allied herself with the less distinguished, who were sitting in the bow.

Rose had a silly laugh and the glottal-stop speech of what has come to be known as Estuary English, but Agatha began to become interested in her. Despite the fact that Rose was probably somewhere in her fifties, she had cultivated a baby-doll appearance. She pouted; her eyelashes, though false, were good; her breasts revealed by a low frilly sundress were excellent; and her long thin legs ending in high-heeled strapped sandals were brown and smooth. She had wrinkles on her neck and round her mouth and eyes, but every movement, every bit of body language seemed to scream out the promise of Good in Bed.

Trevor was besotted with her, and so was the elderly Scotsman, Angus. In conversation it came out that Trevor owned a prosperous plumbing business and that Angus, a recently made friend, was a retired shopkeeper. The quiet couple had taken out books and had started to read and so the conversation went on among Agatha, Rose, Trevor and Angus.

Rose let slip, almost as if by accident, that she was very well read. After every occasional comment, it seemed to Agatha as if she remembered her role of silly endearing woman and quickly returned to it. Had she settled for money? The diamonds on the many rings on her fingers were real.

The voyage was short but pleasant, the sea breeze refreshing. They anchored in Turtle Beach Cove.

They swam from the boat. Agatha was a good swimmer, but she was out of condition and found that the shore was much farther away than it had looked from the yacht. Relieved to have escaped from the others, she floated on her back in the shallow water and dreamed of meeting James, her eyes closed against the burning sun above. And then she floated against a rock. It was a flat rock and it was a nudge she felt rather than a bump, but she struggled to her feet, suddenly terrified, and looked wildly around. She had not yet got over the fright of being knocked unconscious by someone and nearly buried alive during what she considered as 'my last case'.

She could hear her heart thumping. She took several deep breaths and sat down in the green-blue water, which was shallow enough.

The skipper, whose name was Ibraham, was swimming about, making sure none of his passengers drowned or had a heart attack. His wife, who sailed with him, a short, black-haired woman called Ferda, was preparing lunch and the clatter of dishes and glasses floated to Agatha's ears across the water.

Rose's husband, Trevor, was heaving his great bulk, sunburnt now to a nasty salmon-pink, up the ladder at the side of the yacht. He stopped halfway and turned and glared back across the bay.

Agatha looked to see what had caught his attention. Sitting side by side in the water a little away from Agatha were Rose and Olivia's husband, George, giggling about something.

Olivia herself was swimming backwards and forwards with powerful back-arm strokes. Trevor was still halfway up the ladder. The elderly friends of the two women, Harry and Angus, were trying to get back on board the yacht. Harry reached up and tapped Trevor on the back. Trevor turned round and fell back into the water, nearly colliding with the two old men. He began to swim towards his wife. Rose saw him coming and immediately left George and began to swim towards him.

Agatha stayed where she was, enjoying the solitude. She suddenly wished with all her heart that she could forget about James and be free again, free to enjoy a peaceful holiday without being haunted and obsessed by the man. Then she heard herself being hailed from the yacht. Lunch was about to be served. Agatha was reluctant to return. Her brief interest in Rose had fled, leaving her with a feeling of distaste for all her fellow passengers. She swam back and pulled herself up the ladder, conscious of her round stomach. She would need to get herself in shape for James.

Lunch was pleasant: complimentary glasses of wine, good chicken, crisp salad. Pleased as any tourist might be to find she had not been ripped off, Agatha mellowed enough to join Rose, her husband and friend. She noticed, however, that Olivia's husband, George, kept looking over at Rose from his place at the bar. He said something to his wife in an undertone and she answered loudly, 'I don't feel like slumming today.'

When the young meet up on an outing abroad, they exchange addresses at the end of it or arrange to meet in the evening. The middle-aged and elderly, by silent consent, simply part with a nod and a smile. Agatha had enjoyed herself on the sail back, for she had told them all about her detective work and entertained them with highly embroidered stories about how clever she had been.

But she, too, after the yacht had slid into Kyrenia harbour under the shadow of the old castle, simply said goodbye and walked away. Olivia, her husband and friend were all residing at the Dome Hotel. With luck, she would be able to avoid them. She had more important work to do.

She had to find James.

She was reluctant to dine in the hotel that evening, so she checked her guidebook and selected a restaurant called the Grapevine which looked hopeful, and took a taxi the short distance there, not wanting to bother driving. It was a good choice, the restaurant being in the garden of an old Ottoman house. Agatha ordered wine and swordfish kebab and tried not to feel lonely.

The garden was heavy with the scent of jasmine and full of the sound of British voices. It was a great favourite with the British residents, according to a blonde woman called Carol who served her meal. There were evidently a great number of British residents in north Cyprus: they even had their own village outside Kyrenia called Karaman, complete with houses called things like Cobblers, and a British library, and a pub called the Crow's Nest.

Agatha had brought a paperback with her and was trying to read by candlelight when Carol brought her a note. It said simply, 'Come and join us.'

She looked across the restaurant. Just taking their seats at a centre table were Rose, husband and friend, and Olivia, husband and friend. They were smiling and waving in her direction.

Intrigued that such an unlikely combination should get together, Agatha picked up her plate and wine and went to join them.

'Isn't this a surprise?' said Rose. 'There we was, just walking down the street, when my Trevor, he says, he says to me, "Isn't that Olivia?"' Agatha noticed Olivia wince. 'And Georgie says, "Come and join us," so here we all are! Innit *fun!*'

To Agatha's amazement, Olivia seemed to be making an effort to be polite to Rose, Trevor and Angus. It transpired that her husband, George, had recently retired from the Foreign Office, that friend Harry Tembleton was a farmer, and that Olivia herself had heard of Agatha, for the Debenhams had a manor house in Lower Cramber in the Cotswolds.

The wine circulated and Rose grew more animated. It seemed she was a specialist in the double entendre. She had a really filthy laugh, a bar-room laugh, a gin-and-sixty-cigarettes-a-day laugh, which sounded around the restaurant. George crossed his legs under the table and his foot brushed against Rose's leg. He apologized and Rose shrieked with laughter. 'Go on,' she said, giving him a nudge with one thin, pointed elbow. 'I know what you're after!'

Agatha did not think anyone could eat kebab off its skewer in a suggestive manner, but Rose did. Then she, it seemed deliberately, misunderstood the simplest remarks. George said he hoped there wouldn't be another tube strike in London when they got back because he had some business in the City to attend to. 'A boob strike,' cried Rose gleefully. 'Has Olivia stopped your jollies?'

Agatha gave her a bored look and Rose mouthed at her, 'Like Lysistrata.' So vulgar Rose knew her Greek classics, thought Agatha, who had only recently boned up on them herself. And somehow Rose knew that Agatha had rumbled her act.

What was an intelligent woman doing being tied to

the brutish Trevor and a dreary retired shopkeeper like Angus?

Angus was a man of few words and those that he had were delivered in a slow portentous manner. 'Scottish education is the finest in the world, yes,' he said, apropos of nothing. Things like that.

Olivia had a bright smile pinned on her face as she tried to 'draw' everyone out, and did it very well, thought Agatha, although noticing that Olivia could not quite mask that she detested Rose and thought Trevor a boor. She entertained them with a funny story about how the man in the hotel room upstairs had let his bath overrun so that it had seeped down into the ceiling of their room and he refused to admit he was guilty and said they must have left the windows open and let the rain in.

To Agatha's surprise, they all decided to go on an expedition to the Othello Tower in Famagusta the next day and she was urged to join them. They would hire cars. She refused. Tomorrow was James Lacey-hunting day. They had been going to spend their honeymoon at a rented villa outside Kyrenia. She would try to find it.

Trevor insisted on paying the bill, joking that it would be the first time in his life he was a millionaire as he pulled out wads and wads of Turkish lira. Agatha refused a lift, deciding to walk back to the hotel. She was streetwise enough to know that she was safe, and Rose, who had arrived a week before her, had told her with a tinge of regret in her voice that there was no danger of

261

getting your bottom pinched. Rose had also said that there was also no danger of getting your handbag snatched, or of being cheated by shopkeepers. So Agatha strolled down past the town hall and along Kyrenia's main street.

And then she saw James.

He was ahead of her, walking with that achingly familiar long, easy, loping stride of his. She let out a strangled cry and began to run on her high heels. He turned a corner next to a supermarket. She ran ahead, calling his name, but when she, too, turned the corner, he had disappeared. She had once seen the French film, *Les Enfants du Paradis*, and this felt like the last scene where the hero desperately tries to catch up with his beloved.

A Turkish soldier blocked her way and asked her anxiously in broken English if he could help her.

'My friend. I saw my friend,' babbled Agatha, staring up the side street. 'Is there a hotel along there?'

'No, that is Little Turkey. Ironmongers, cafés, no hotel. Sorry.'

But Agatha ploughed on, peering at deserted shops, stumbling over potholes. Then she saw a light shining out from a laundry called White Rose, Beyaz Gül in Turkish. A man in shirt-sleeves was working at a dry-cleaning machine. Agatha pushed open the door and went in.

'Can I help you?' he asked.

He was a small man with a clever, attractive face.

262

'You speak English?'

'Yes, I worked in England for some time as a nurse. My wife, Jackie, is English.'

'Oh, good. Look, I saw this friend of mine come along here a moment ago, but he's disappeared.'

'I don't know where he could have been going. Sit down. I'm called Bilal.'

'I'm Agatha.'

'Would you like a coffee? I'm working late because it's cooler at night. Trying to get as much done as I can when I can.'

Agatha felt suddenly tired, weepy and disappointed.

'No, I think I'll go back to the hotel.'

'North Cyprus is very small,' he said sympathetically. 'You're bound to run into your friend sooner or later. Do you know the Grapevine?'

'Yes, I had dinner there this evening.'

'You should ask there. All the British end up there sooner or later.'

For some reason, Bilal, although probably somewhere in his mid-forties, reminded her of Bill Wong.

'Thanks,' she said, getting to her feet again.

'Tell me the name of your friend,' said Bilal, 'and maybe I can find something out for you.'

'James Lacey, retired colonel, fifties, tall with very blue eyes, and black hair going grey.'

'Are you at the Dome?'

'Yes.'

'Write down your name for me. I've a terrible memory.'

263

Agatha wrote down her name. 'A laundry is an odd business for a nurse,' she commented.

'I'm used to it now,' said Bilal. 'At first I made some awful mistakes. They would give me those Turkish wedding dresses covered in sequins and I'd put them in the dry-cleaning machine, but the sequins were made of plastic and they all melted. And then they come down from the mountains with the suit they bought about forty years ago covered in olive oil and wine and expect me to give it back to them looking like new.' He gave a comical sigh.

'In any case, can I come back and see you?' asked Agatha.

'Any time. We can have coffee.'

Feeling somewhat cheered, she left. She wandered round more streets. Men sat outside cafés playing backgammon, music blared, half-key Turkish music, sad and haunting.

At last she gave up the search and returned to the hotel. She thought she should have gone back to the Grapevine. Maybe tomorrow.

The next morning she awoke heavy-eyed and sweating profusely. She showered and put on a loose cotton dress and flat sandals. She ate a light breakfast of cheese-filled pastry and then went on impulse into the car-rental office.

'Did you by any chance rent a car to a Mr Lacey?' she asked.

'Yes, I did,' said the man behind the desk. He stood up and shook hands with her. 'It's Mrs Raisin, isn't it? I'm Mehmet Chavush. In fact, Mr Lacey renewed his rental this morning.'

'When?'

'An hour ago.'

'Do you know ... did he say where he was going today?'

'Mr Lacey said something abut going to Gazimağusa.'

Agatha looked blank.

'You probably know it as Famagusta,' he said helpfully.

'How do I get there?'

'Drive up past the post office.' He led her to a map on the wall. 'Here. And then take this road up over the mountains. It will lead you down on to the dual carriageway on the Famagusta road. You might have come that way from the airport.'

'Yes, I think I did.'

Agatha set off. Round the roundabout, past the post office, very much an architectural reminder of British colonial days, and so out towards the mountains. The heat was tremendous, but for once she barely noticed it. The air-conditioning in the car was working – just.

The mountains were bare and stark, scorched from the forest fires of the year before. She recognized the army chicanes as she came down from the mountains. A soldier on guard duty beside the road waved to her and gave her the thumbs-up sign and Agatha's heart began

265

to lift with hope. Ahead lay Famagusta and James. And then she thought, I should have asked for the registration number of his car. All the rented cars looked much the same, with red licence plates to denote they were rented. And Mehmet probably had a record of James's address.

She carefully observed the speed limit through two villages and then the Famagusta road, which follows the line where the old railway used to run, stretched straight out in front of her across the Mesaoria Plain, straight as an arrow, and no speed limit.

Agatha put her foot down hard and flew like a bird towards the far horizon.